THE DEVIL'S ANGEL

Kingdawud Mujahid Burgess

THE DEVIL'S ANGEL

by

Kingdawud Mujahid Burgess

SIMMS BOOKS PUBLISHING

SIMMS BOOKS PUBLISHING

Publishers Since 2012

Published By Simms Books Publishing

Jonesboro, GA

Library of Congress Cataloging in Publication Data

Kingdawud Mujahid Burgess

The Devil's Angel

ISBN: 978-0-692-42836-8

Printed in the United States of America

Book Arrangement by Simms Books Publishing

Cover by Urias Brown, Michael Shield Studios-urias@michaelshieldstudio.com

ACKNOWLEDGEMENTS

Special Thanks to my Queen Najla Alasmi who has held me down for thirteen long hard trying years. She has loved me from the moment we laid eyes upon each other and if it wasn't for her I would have no mercy for many people. She taught me how to love, gave me a reason to be happy and blessed me to find inner peace. Dear Omani Queen, if ever we were to break apart I would truly be devastated. The rarest jewel I have been given in life would be missing from my crown. Just striving to be half as smart as you, you have made me a brilliant man.

To my aunt Portia Etheridge, I love you so much and you have always loved me even when others did not. Aunt Reberta Motley, you have always found space for me in your life and because of you I have always felt whole. Jr and Lilly my two siblings, who have never made it, seem as if it was a burden for me to be in your lives, I love you. To my cousin Lafeyette Nelson you are truly my blood brother I love you.

1

FOR AS LONG AS HE COULD REMEMBER, all he had thought about was taking a trip to Chicago, in hopes of finding the father he had never even spoken to.

He wanted so badly to know why the man that gave him life didn't feel it necessary to be involved in his life at all.

His mother, who wanted nothing to do with her cheating ex-husband, or the city of Chicago which she had migrated to at the age of 14, had told him many bad stories about his father, which made him want to have absolutely nothing to do with the man.

That was before he himself went to jail where he had a lot of time to think about if in fact he really did want to know the man who gave him life.

He had come to the conclusion that no child deserves to have to live not knowing where and who they come from.

Against his mother's suggestion, he was finally going to find out who his father was and why he had selfishly abandoned him and his mother so many years ago. Just seeing Chicago, the city of his birth, had him very excited. He could feel his heart pounding away in his chest as his palms began to sweat, causing him to wipe them dry on his pant legs.

"My, My, this trip is long," said the elderly lady who had been busy knitting a blanket beside him for the entire ride. She looked over at him with a smile on her face.

"I guess I should have let my son put me on the plane but I am so afraid of flying for some reason," turning her face away from him to look down at the quilt that she had nearly finished.

Denardo, who was fearful of missing his first sight of the enchanted city sky lights, reluctantly turned to look down at her very briefly.

"Ohh, you're looking for them huge lights in the sky like everyone else, right? If you ask me, this damned city is so overrated," she exclaimed, as she tucked away the quilt that had fallen to the floor next to her feet.

Denardo wasn't ignoring her but instead paying more attention to the side of the highway which was decorated with fine sculpture of lifelike sea creatures. He inhaled deeply as his heart began to strike away at his chest even harder.

"That's how they get you, baby, all these fancy roads and bright lights leading up to the darkest and deadliest city on earth."

Upon hearing her say what she had just said to him, he burst into laughter.

"There's your City of Dreams," pointing toward 55th Street, where the Sky Lights of the City of Chicago began to come to life.

As he turned his head to look, he felt as if he was in an enchanted world of Kings and Queens, a place like an Egyptian City. The enormous buildings and vibrant lights made Chicago look like the loveliest city on earth.

"This is a beautiful paradise!" He yelled out.

"I don't know what the hell you been smoking on baby, but Chicago is far from a paradise!" She answered back sarcastically. "Beautiful. Yes, but deadly as hell."

She shook her head. "You're just like everyone else. You see something that looks good and you automatically think you're looking at a sparking diamond. Remember this here baby:

"Everything that looks good ain't good for you,"

Pointing toward the three tallest buildings that sat over the top of the city she asked,

"You see that building right there?"

"Yes," nodding his head.

"That's the *Daily Center* and the other one's the *Willis Tower* and the others are the *Trump Towers*."

He continued to stare up at the buildings as if they were part of a magical kingdom.

As the bus exited the highway it came upon Roosevelt Street, making its way over to Taylor Street where the Greyhound bus station stood.

Once inside the bus station, the bus pulled up to the building and stopped.

"People, this is Taylor Street Station, the second from the last stop that this bus will be making. Please remember to gather all of your belongings before getting off and welcome to Chicago," echoed a voice over the loud speaker.

Denardo watched as nearly all of the people of the bus stood and began gathering their things.

As the old woman stood to her feet so did he.

"Is this your stop as well?"

"No ma'am, I was gonna help you take your bags inside if you needed me to."

The woman smiled as she gathered her only bag from under the seat.

"I'm not as old as I look, baby and you'd be surprised," giving him as smile as she made her way down the aisle.

She continued on as he watched her from behind and before long she was off the bus and disappeared from his sight.

As he took his seat, he began to wonder to himself if she was his grandmother on his father's side. For a moment he drifted off into his thoughts until he heard the echoing voice of the bus driver over the loudspeaker.

"We will be reaching our final stop in about fifteen more minutes, ladies and gentlemen. Remember to gather all your belongings and again, Welcome to the City of Chicago."

Denardo reached into his pocket, grabbing a hold of his phone. Looking over the screen he noticed he had several missed calls from his mother and his Aunt Sandy, who he would be staying with.

He placed the phone up to his ear and listened as it rung.

After the tenth ring, he hung up the phone placing it back into his pocket.

He figured that his Aunt Sandy must be in the shower or already on the train and was not in range, could've lost the signal on the train.

He would try her again once he got outside Jefferson Manor. He thought about calling his mother but wanted to wait until he had something to tell her.

The bus pulled up to the terminal and stopped, allowing him and the rest of the passengers to make their way off.

As he stepped out, the frigid air seemed to hit him all at once. He placed his bags down on the ground at his feet and pulled his hat down over his ears. He then zipped his coat up and made his way over towards the huge crowd of men who appeared to be crack heads trying to hustle someone for a few dollars.

"Hey my man, I can get you to where you're going." A dingy looking man who wore all black said as he threw his hands up to get his attention.

Denardo looked over to the few cars that sat in the parking lot, none of which were official cab cars.

"Naw, I'm good."

As he made his way over to the highway, he spotted a yellow cab making its way down the street towards him. He stepped out into the street, directly in the lane of the cab, which caused it to stop abruptly.

"You stupid mutha fucker! What are you doing? Trying to get yourself killed?" Yelled the driver, whose English wasn't very good while sticking his head out of the window.

Denardo knew that he had found real cab driver and without saying another word grabbed a hold of the door and jumped into the back of the man's cab.

"Drive and don't stop until I tell you to"

"What? Are you freaking crazy or what?" Said the man as he looked back at him with angry eyes, seeing how he had no choice but to drive off.

"Take me to a mall so I can get some clothes that won't get me shot at around here."

The driver looked back at him through his rearview mirror and said,

"I take it that you're not from around here?"

"Naw and what gave it away, my accent?"

"No, the fact that you're black and you was stupid enough to jump in the cab with a Spanish man. That's what gave it away." The cab driver responded, turning his attention back to the road in front of him.

"Look, I'm headed to Jefferson Manor Building 412 Apartment 77, and here is two hundred and fifty dollars if you are willing to take me there," Denardo said as he held his hand out with the money.

The driver took the money placing it into his pocket.

"I thought so,"

"Look, all areas in this city are not neutral and if I get caught up in 'The Manor,' I'm good as dead, so your money don't mean shit to me."

"I'll take you there only if I can drop you off a block away."

"That's cool; now take me to the closest mall so I can get a new set of clothes,"

After driving for another five minutes, the cab made a left off the highway into a huge shopping center that was filled with stores.

"Have you ever seen so many shops in one area?"

"Naw not this many," Denardo said as he stared mesmerized at all the stores that appeared to stretch for more than a mile or better in both directions.

"So where are you gonna go shopping, because as you can see many of the people who own these shops have not even arrived yet to open them to the public."

Denardo saw a beautiful woman standing out in front of the Armani Exchange and he quickly told the driver to stop.

The cab came to a quick stop allowing for him to make his way out the vehicle.

"Wait here for me; I'll be back in like twenty minutes or less."

He then travelled over to the curb making his way off the street and he didn't stop until he was making his way through the doors of the Armani Exchange

2

AS HE MADE HIS WAY TOWARDS THE BACK EXIT OF CLUB HELL, one of many real estate investments that he owned throughout the city of Chicago, Felipia, or The Devil as he was known, blew a cloud of marijuana smoke from his lungs.

The eight men who consisted of his entourage surrounded him so closely that had he been any smaller it would have been impossible to see him at all.

Spiney, his top lieutenant, held the glass door on the right open, allowing the first two men in the detail to lead the way outside, as The Devil trailed not far behind.

After making sure there was no apparent danger anywhere nearby, the six men who were standing near the three black Yukon trucks parked in the alley motioned to the entourage who then proceeded to escort their boss across the street to the red Bentley Coupe GT that awaited him

Once The Devil was in the GT and the door safely secured behind him, Spiney ordered the other men back to their cars, as he hopped into the passenger seat of the Bentley next to The Devil.

"Spiney, see if Sleepy and Manny have dropped that stuff off at the new spot that Perrish just opened up, off the Danryan."

Spiney removed his phone from his pocket placing it up to his ear. He said a few words in Spanish, and then hung up. As soon as he hung up, his phone rung and he answered it saying,

"Who the Hell is this?"

After listening for a while he hung up the phone.

"So did they go past the shop to check on her or not?" Felipia asked, while turning to look at the three Yukons that trailed them in his rear view mirror.

"I'm trying to see what the hell is going on right now," pressing send on his phone.

As the two sat reclined in the Bentley another entourage of The Devil's Disciples who had already driven ahead were stopping traffic on every street in front of them to make sure no one got close enough to Felipia's vehicle to try to assassinate him.

Spiney hung up his phone then looked over at Felipia saying,

"We got a problem."

"What type of problem, a big one or a small one?"

"Well, actually we got two tiny problems and a medium sized problem."

"Can it wait? You know I promised Perrish that I would take her out of town later today and I was gonna actually go by the shop now and surprise her."

"Well, I just spoke to Flaco Flame who is somewhere up near O'Hare Airport, with no coat, no money or no shoes. Apparently he got robbed."

The look on Felipia's face said it all. Spiney could tell that his boss was angry as hell.

"Who would be stupid enough to rob someone who's under my protection, and what the hell is this idiot still doing in the city when he was supposed to have been on a plane over an hour ago?"

"Get Manny and Sleepy on the phone."

"Well that was them I just hung up the phone with. According to Flaco Flame, Sleepy and your other little cousin Manny are the ones that robbed him."

From the look on The Devil's face Spiney could tell that he had just gone from angry to mad.

He smiles to himself knowing that Manny and Sleepy *(who had run around doing basically whatever they wanted in the city based on the fact that they were the cousins of the head of The Devil's Disciples)* were finally about to see what it felt like to be humbled.

"So what do Sleepy and Manny have to say?" Felipia asked as he turned his head to look over at Spiney.

"You can ask them yourself; there they are right up ahead of us."

When the car was right next to the Cadillac with Manny and Sleepy sitting on the hood, it stopped, allowing for Spiney and Felipia to exit the vehicle.

"Well, well, what do we have ourselves here?" Spiney said, placing the pump shotgun he held in his right

14

hand across his chest while looking into both Manny and Sleepy's eyes.

The Devil walked up to the front of the car and got right up in Manny's face.

"As long as these artists or anyone else is up under the protection of The Devil, they are never to be touched by anybody! When people who I have sworn to protect are harmed it makes me look weak!". "

Manny looked over at Sleepy and before he could turn his head back in the direction where Felipia stood he was hit with two quick blows that caused him to slide across the hood of the car onto the ground. Felipia began to kick him mercilessly as Sleepy, who knew that he was next, watched on in fear.

The Devil stopped stumping Manny and turned his attention to Sleepy.

"So what happened?"

For a moment Sleepy hesitated to speak, but when he saw Spiney pointing the shotgun at his chest he looked into Felipia's eyes and said,

"This guy is a fucking studio gangster who is talking shit to us like he's some big shot killer. He was making all types of threats and stuff like he was a gangster so we decided to show him that he was a bitch."

"We beat him like the woman he is and took his money, jewelry and clothes, putting him outside in the freezing cold in his underwear." Manny added.

"What was we supposed to do, let some bitch ass nigga front on us like that?"

"Yeah, that's exactly what you was supposed to do. I wouldn't give a damned if the kid told you to suck his dick. If he's under my protection the chief of police or the Mayor of this city isn't authorized to touch him!"

Felipia grabbed Sleepy around his neck and began choking him.

"Bring him over here," Spiney said, motioning to the Disciples behind him.

Out of nowhere the barefooted, naked, shivering Flaco appeared and made his way over to the Cadillac.

"What do you want to do now Flaco?" The Devil asked, looking back at him, as Sleepy gasped for air.

"Flaco!" Spiney yelled, which caused him to look up.

"The Devil wants to know what is it that you want done to these two clowns, Manny and Sleepy."

"I just wanna go home," he said, looking away from Spiney and The Devil.

"Give him his jewelry and money now and give him both your clothes and shoes," The Devil said, releasing Sleepy from his grip.

Quickly the two men emptied their pockets and took off the jewelry they had taken from Flaco Flame.

"Get this stuff and put on any of these clothes you like."

Both Manny and Sleepy began to strip naked in front of him.

Flaco gathered his belongings, and then pulled on Manny's jeans and shirt while placing Sleepy's shoes and socks on his feet.

"Now beat the hell out of both of them before I let Spiney blow a hole in your scared ass!"

He looked up at The Devil hoping he was joking, but once he felt the steel of the shotgun on the back of his head he began swinging on Sleepy and Manny and didn't stop until he was out of breath.

Felipia knew that it was an honor for Sleepy and Manny to say that The Devil smacked them both around, but to be beaten by a lame duck who was scared of its own shadow would be something that would haunt the both of them for as long as they lived.

3

ANY MAN WHO HAD EVER LAID EYES ON PERRISH HAMILTON believed themselves to have seen an angel. There was no doubt that her beauty was extremely mesmerizing, so mesmerizing that some believed it to be her only flaw as well.

She stood at the back of her store, which was part Armani Exchange and part Fresh Feet, the only store in the city of Chicago that made custom fitting designer shoes. As she shuffled through the papers on her desk she heard his voice calling out for help, causing her to stop what she was doing and make a getaway from her desk.

She exited her office and headed across the floor of her shoe store over to the Armani Exchange side towards the front of it. Once Denardo saw her come through the glass door that separated the two stores, his heart dropped.

"O, I'm sorry, we usually don't have customers this early," she said, smiling as she looked into his eyes. "May I help you with something?" Perrish stood there placing her soft flawless hands upon her voluptuous hips.

"I think I'm in love."

"Excuse me?!" she said, sounding confused by the statement he had made.

"That's a powerful statement and being that it was so easy for you to say, I doubt that you really understand the meaning of love," she said, batting her huge oval-shaped crystal like grey eyes.

"You've never heard of love at first sight?"

Looking down at her well-manicured feet nestled in a pair of size five ostrich open-toed Fendi spaghetti-strapped pumps. They were black and beige, matching her skirt which ended right below her knees.

"You're not in love, you're just lusting and I would appreciate it if you stopped." Perrish turned to walk away.

He wanted to say something to make her stop; upon seeing the shape of her booty which was bouncing as she pertly strutted away, he was left speechless. He instantly became hard as he watched her make her way back over to the door. He continued to watch her in admiration as her soft silky hair, slightly curled at the bottom, bounced with the rhythm of her voluptuous soft tender booty.

"Please stop. I didn't mean any disrespect. I know you must be constantly complimented on your beauty by both men and women, but I think your soul is calling out to me."

Perrish stopped in her tracts, releasing the door handle as she turned around.

"Listen, I know this sounds weird but you and I are meant to be and I know it."

She blushed, looking down at her toes which could be seen through the front of her shoes.

"You don't even know me to be saying the things that you are saying, so don't be surprised when I tell you that you sound crazy," batting her lovely eyes at him.

"Besides, how do you know that I'm not already somebody's soul mate or wife?"

"No disrespect, but I believe that if you are married then you did it for all the wrong reasons. Like you said, I don't know you, but at the same time I know you so well. None of us truly know the Creator of Heaven and Earth but we believe in HIM as if HE walked us to school everyday. Look Miss, all I'm saying is this, if you have felt as if something in your life was missing, or that you needed to be somewhere but didn't know where that was, then you have to know that place is with me."

Perrish, deeply affected by his words, looked away from him to keep from shedding a tear. Here it was that a stranger was telling her how much he loved her without even truly knowing her, when the man she loved acted as if he couldn't even find the time to call her back or take her out once a month. She inhaled deeply while looking back over at him.

"So what makes you so sure of yourself and what makes you so sure of me?" Looking down at the five carat diamond and platinum ring on her finger.

"How hard is it to buy somebody a diamond?" He asked.

As he stared at her, she studied the ring that The Devil had given her over three years ago.

"Men buy rings for women just to put them on a lay-away plan, but when a man truly knows that he belongs with a woman and when he knows what he's got, he won't risk losing you and will want everybody to know that you belong to him."

"Think about this for a minute…When we spend our time working for something we want our name on the check and we want proof of ownership on whatever it is we buy. We want our names on our diplomas, our house notes and our car titles. Even though people don't like getting bills, they still want to see their name on the bill as proof of responsibility or to show who's really in charge."

"Wow" she said, smiling.

He continued.

"Let me finish before you start doubting me or getting all sarcastic."

She made a face that clearly showed her dimples, and then gave him a sign with her hand to keep going.

"Look at everything that man values, diamonds, gold, oil, steel; these things men will risk his life and travel to the center of the earth, and when he gets what he is after he wants everyone to know of his accomplishments. He wants the recognition by being paid for what he did. With the same money a man makes off the entire world's precious metals and minerals, he spends this wealth on a woman of his choice as a token to show her how much she truly makes him happy. It's hard to pan for gold or drill for oil, but men still do it, so why would a man who values a woman or women in general not lay claim to his woman. A woman will carry his name and build his legacy while raising his children."

Everything he was saying had her in deep thought, and the more he talked the more she realized that Felipia, whom she had known since she was fifteen, didn't truly love her.

"Your words are very compassionate and poetic but how do I know that what you have said to me is not just another poem you wrote and perfected to steal me or another woman from her man, maybe only for one night?"

He made his way across the floor over to her, and then grabbed hold of her hands while looking deep into her eyes. Tears began to form in his eyes.

"I know how you feel because I feel the same way. We are so busy guessing if the move we make will be the right one that we fail to take the chances we need to take to find true love. I'm not perfect, but together we can be. If I cannot promise you nothing else I can promise you that I'll love and cherish the very ground you walk on in life and in death."

Perrish lowered her head and that's when he kissed her. At first she was startled and shocked and then her mind told her to push him away, but the energy she felt coming from his body embraced her and made her feel like she was the safest woman on earth.

"And for all I've done for you, this is how you repay me, you dirty whorish slut!"

The sound of Felipia's voice startled her, causing her to pull back from Denardo. In shock she looked over at her fiancé of three years as pain and anger ran through his eyes and face.

"Felipia!" Perrish approached slowly, arms and hands outreached trying to calm him.

She looked at Denardo then made her way over to The Devil. The Devil, who was accompanied by Spiney, continued to look into Denardo's eyes as if he wanted to kill him.

He had always known how beautiful Perrish was but at that very moment she appeared to him more beautiful than ever. Seeing her with another man had finally made him see her for whom and what she was, but his pride and the power he possessed would not allow her or the man she was kissing to live to tell about what they'd done.

"Felipia, baby, it is not what it looks like," she cried, looking up at him while grabbing his hand.

He pulled his hand away from her and struck her across her face so hard; she flew up against a rack of clothes then tumbled to the floor.

Without hesitation Denardo rushed toward him and as he did Spiney reached for his gun while The Devil began to cock his leg back to kick Perrish in her face. Denardo got to Spiney before he could pull his gun from the small of his back and hit him with six straight punches, causing him to fall.

He jumped on top of him and continued to beat him. While he was beating Spiney, The Devil, three times Perrish's size, was kicking her as if she were a soccer ball. Denardo got off Spiney and grabbed hold of The Devil and the two of them began to wrestle. Denardo, lighter than The Devil, knew he couldn't let him slam him. He got loose from Felipia and struck him across his face twice causing Felipia's knees to buckle.

"No!" Perrish, who was bleeding from her mouth and nose yelled, trying to get Denardo to stop beating her finance.

"Bitch Ima kill both of you for your disloyalty!" He roared reaching for the forty caliber automatic hand gun strapped on the right hand side of his waist.

Denardo struck him again, grabbing his hand as they both began to wrestle with each other for the gun. As Perrish screamed for them to stop, the gun came out and hit the floor near The Devil's right foot. He bent over to grab it. Denardo kneed him in the nose then grabbed the gun before he could recover it. When he got the gun in hand he noticed Spiney again conscious reaching for his weapon.

"Watch out!"

Perrish yelled to Denardo, who pointed the gun at Spiney's chest and fired. The three shots he fired killed Spiney instantly. He then turned the gun on Felipia and fired five shots, striking him in his chest, stomach, and neck. Perrish, who was crying, screamed

"Noooooo!" while watching The Devil close his eyes and slump down to the floor-dead.

The outside window of the Armani Exchange burst when two of The Devil disciples opened fire on it trying to shoot Denardo.

"Get down!" He yelled, running over to Perrish who he tackled to the floor.

They squirmed over to the side of the wall in order not to get hit by the rapid oncoming gun fire meant for the both of them. Perrish looked over at Felipia's body. She never thought that he would ever put his hands on her. As she continued to stare over at him, Denardo rose up and fired on the door the two men were coming through. The shots struck one of the men and shattered the glass.

The sound of shattering glass was nearly muffled by the sound of the loud gunshots.

He tried to look up but had to keep low to keep from being shot.

"We can't get out that way," Perrish said, grabbing hold of his hand.

"Follow me!"

Crawling across the floor over toward Felipia's body.

"What are you doing?" Denardo asked as he watched her remove a platinum and diamond bracelet from around Felipia's wrist.

She placed the bracelet inside her bra, and then grabbed Denardo's other hand.

"Come on!"

They both ran across the store floor. They continued to move at a fast pace until they reached the back door. Perrish opened it and exited the building with him right behind her.

In a small gated parking lot directly behind the store waited her car, a burgundy Ferrari V-12 FF bomb. She ran over to the front door and opened it as he entered the passenger door. She started it up, drove through the gate and out the alley that lead out to the main street.

"My God! My God!" She said, looking unbraided and afraid.

"You're not shot, are you?"

"I'm ok. No what I am saying I'm okay? I just watched you kill the man I love!"

"How do you think I am?"

"My God! My God! This is terrible! What the hell are we gonna do now?"

"We'll be ok, just stop tripping."

"O, now I'm tripping?!"

Perrish drew her arm back then started swinging at Denardo's face.

She struck him and he didn't even try to block the next three times she hit him.

"Are you happy now?!"

Denardo had taken more than he could take; grabbing a hold of her arms as he allowed the sting from the last two punches to go away.

"You have no idea what type of trouble you have just put both of us in, do you?"

"Naw, but we got the rest of our lives together so I'm sure that one day you will find the time to tell me."

"Boy, you just don't get it. You just ruined any chance of a future that we might have had together. That guy you just killed was the founder of The Devil's Disciples, which is the worst Spanish gang in America. These guys won't hesitate to kill everybody you know."

"Why are you still flipping out? Those guys don't even know me. None of my family is in this city and I doubt they wanna come to New York and bump heads with the Crips and Bloods that run my city streets."

"What about my family, haw? Did you think of that?" she asked, rolling her eyes at him.

"Listen! We can't take back what has already happened. That guy is dead and he ain't coming back."

"Yeah and you made sure of that," she said, raising her voice as she made a right hand turn.

"Today was the first day of my life and the best one I have lived so far in my twenty five years on earth. I waited all my life to come to Chicago and something told me that it was something here I needed to find. I thought that thing might have been the father I never knew but when I saw you I knew instantly why I had traveled to this city, and I don't regret that for one moment. Sorry about what happened, but if I had to do it all over again just to be sitting next to you, then I would."

His words calmed her. He could tell from the way her facial expression changed.

She inhaled deeply, and then exhaled.

"Ok. Ok. Look! We have to get out of this city quick before these guys find us."

For the next ten minutes they road in silence, not even daring to look at each other. He reached over and grabbed hold of her hand as his heart pounded away at his chest. She made him as nervous as he ever felt around a woman.

"Everything will be ok and if you haven't noticed by now, I will die protecting you."

A tear fell from her eye and he reached over to wipe it from her cheek. She turned and looked at him.

"Are you crying for your fiancé?"

He asked in a calm voice, and without saying a word she shook her head in the positive.

"So were ya'll getting married or was he your boyfriend?"

She wiped the tears from her eyes and cleared her throat.

"He was neither. Felipia was more like a father to me if anything. I met him when I was only fifteen and he helped put me through medical school. He always wanted the best for me."

"So he wasn't your soon-to-be husband?"

"No,"

"So why the hell are you so heartbroken over him?"

"Once upon a time in my life he gave me a reason to live. My entire family is heavily involved in the streets. All six of my brothers except for the youngest have been killed by gang related violence. Felipia took care of me and made me know that I was somebody when the women around me were consumed by men of the streets who just wanted to use and abuse them for every inch of whatever it was they had to offer. He didn't allow me to get sucked into that way of life so I will always be grateful to him. He was married so he never tried to have sex with me. He wanted me to know that a man really wanted me for more than my looks and what I had between my thighs."

"So you mean to tell me that the meanest Spanish gang in America was run by a gentle giant who was also playing the role of Captain Save-a-Whore?"

Perrish cocked her arm back and swung a blow at him that nearly took his head off.

"O, I'm so sorry baby. I didn't mean you. I was just saying that a man in his position usually enjoys all the fast women he can run though being that they literally throw themselves at him all day. With a nick name The Devil, I would have figured he'd be a little different."

"That's what I'm telling you...he was The Devil with everyone but me. I don't know, for some reason he treated me like royalty."

"That's because he seen you for who you truly are. I guess he wasn't stupid at all."

"No, he was very clever, and very dangerous to those he needed to keep in line. Before I even met him, I had heard his name a couple times."

"From who, the little girls you knew who wanted to have sex with him?"

"No."

"My father was a chief in the Gangster Disciples and that's why so many of my brothers, his sons ended up getting killed. I have heard The Devil's name mentioned by my father and my brothers who all wanted to kill him. For a long time I hated Felipia and didn't even know him. I guess I felt he might have had something to do with the murders of my brothers so I intentionally made myself available to him in order to kill him."

Denardo was shocked by what he heard her say, and looked at her very carefully.

"Everything that looks good ain't good for you," she said, checking the cars in her rear view mirror.

"Damn, that's the second time I heard that since I've been in Chicago," shaking his head.

"So what happened?"

"What do you mean what happened?"

"How'd you go from wanting to kill him to loving him?"

"We'll, he never had sex with me no matter how much I tried to seduce him. He always made his Disciples respect me. He also eventually told me that he knew what I wanted from him."

As she talked, he listened and tried to visualize everything she told him.

"So did he have anything to do with the murders of your brothers?"

"If he did, I can assure you that you wouldn't have had the chance to kill him today.

"He told me that he knew I wanted to kill him over a business deal that had gone wrong between him and my father which caused my father to try to kill him. He told me he never even retaliated against my family at all."

"And you believed that?"

"Yes," she said, raising her voice.

"He had the men who had my father and brothers assassinated, killed as well. The Gangsters were having a problem within their own organization. My father was acting Chief at the time and when my father and brothers failed to kill Felipia and several of their other enemies, the King of the gangsters ordered their assassinations."

"So why didn't you go after the King?"

"The GD King is untouchable. Only certain people are allowed close enough to even hear his voice. To many men, even his enemies, he is considered a God in a man's body."

"So what happened after Felipia found out your true intentions?"

"He made the man who assassinated my brothers and father suffers for days while I watched. I knew that he had the right men because my brother would tell me of how the men on the street would speak about the King's most loyal and trust worthy assassins just going missing. At first everyone believed that the King had had them killed off as well, but when they got word that he hadn't, I knew that the men Felipia had tortured and killed in front of me were the men. I remember their faces vividly."

"I truly began to believe him when pictures of the two men were being worn on T-shirts by the GD's to honor them."

"So you and Felipia never had sex?"

"I told you, he was married." He feared that his son Felipia Junior or "Little Devil would have killed me if he thought I was a threat to his succeeding his father to the throne once he retired or was killed, so in order not to put my life in danger or to cause his best friend, successor and only son to turn against him, he asked me to be patient with our love for each other.

"And you went for that? I mean that might have meant you waiting to be with him for an eternity?"

Perrish looked at him as if he had no idea what it was he was talking about but deep down inside she knew that the chance of her being with Felipia was nearly impossible without the bloodshed of so many which may have included hers as well.

"It was going fine until you showed up" she said, with a frown while making a left-hand turn."

"I guess it was. Who in their right mind would try to steal you away from The Devil? Who in their right mind would try to be with a woman that has a boyfriend and family that were killers? I'm surprised that you are not a virgin because they are so protective. When I first saw you I wondered to myself how a woman so beautiful existed in such an ugly world, but now I realize that you don't exist in this world, you control this world. You are The Devil's Angel."

"Don't call me that!"

Pointing her finger in his face

"You know nothing about me, so stop being judgmental."

"So what now? What about me? Are you gonna hand me over to Little Devil or the Disciples?"

"Are you stupid or something? Those men were shooting at me as well."

"Nobody but you and I know exactly what happened, so as far as Little Devil is concerned, I was responsible for the death of The Devil, which means that he is probably already trying to have me found and killed. Regardless of what you may think about me, I would never put your life in danger when you just risked everything for me without even truly knowing who I am."

"So where the hell are we going now, we need to get out of this city ASAP?"

"I'm going to get some leverage."

"What leverage?"

"This key unlocks a safe that has over eleven million dollars inside of it and I know that to get that money back, Little Devil will be willing to hear what I have to say."

"Eleven million dollars! He trusted you with eleven million dollars?"

"He trusted me with his life and the life of his family. I basically raised his eight year old daughter Ayana, who loves me more than she loves her own mother."

The car turned left on I55 and continued straight until they were a few blocks from Humble Park. He looked around at the ghetto housing and all the Spanish gangsters standing around with evil on their faces as if they were waiting for a war to jump off.

"I haven't seen a black person yet, and I'm assuming that's because our kind is not welcomed around here."

"You'll be ok, just stay inside the car. The windows are tinted so they can't even see whose inside."

"You're playing a very dangerous game."

Looking out of his window at a crowd of thugs with tattoos covering their entire faces.

She pulled to the curb across the street from where they stood and opened her door stepping out.

"You need to tell yourself that."

Perrish looked back at Denardo with a look of distain as she closed the door quickly. She began walking up the sidewalk as he watched.

All of the men and women she passed on her way up the sidewalk either smiles at her or bowed their heads as if to honor her, which was very surprising to Denardo who watched her every step.

"She was The Devil's Angel after all," he thought as he stared at her behind (which even in a perilous situation caused him to become aroused). Everything about her was flawless and if looks could kill… "Well, looks did kill," he thought to himself.

He watched the men who would surely want him dead once they found out what had happened. They paced back and forth past the car as his heart pounded away in his chest.

He looked back toward where Perrish had traveled and when he didn't see her anymore he began to panic.

Was she really going to get eleven million dollars or was she going to make a deal with Little Devil to save her own life, he wondered.

"How stupid could I have been," he wondered to himself.

He thought about leaving, but deep in his heart he wanted to believe everything she had told him. He wanted to believe that the events that had just unfolded had happened for a reason. He wanted to believe that every moment he lived had guided him to that very moment in time.

The parking lot inside the Armani Exchange and the sidewalk outside was covered with Chicago police investigating the shooting death of one of their biggest gang crime lords.

"Detective Five, come over here, will ya?"

Detective Brass of homicide said to the small bald-headed brown-skinned man to his right near the window of the Armani Exchange. Five made his way across the room over to where Brass was standing.

"What is it?" He asked, looking down at Felipia's body.

"I'm trying to figure out why the leader of an all-Spanish gang would be in an all-black part of town that his gang has been warring with for years."

"Have you seen the woman that owns this joint?"

"Naw," Brass said, looking over the store completely.

"Well if you ever see her you'll understand why anybody would go into their enemy's turf."

"Doctor Hamilton is not only very well-educated and attractive, but she is very wealthy as well men will give their big toe to get next to her."

"So where the hell is this Doctor Hamilton?"

"That's exactly what I was wondering myself," Five said, scratching his head.

"Do we have any witnesses yet?" Brass asked looking over the faces of the other detectives who stood inside the store.

"If I can find a rat in this neighborhood I'll buy it cheese for the rest of its life, which I'm sure won't be very long at all," Five said, making his way toward the front of the store.

He looked out into the parking lot at the faces of the men who looked back with disdain on their faces. He wondered to himself if he was staring the killer in the face at that very moment.

"We can't get into the store now that the detectives are in there," Sleepy said, looking over at Five from the passenger seat of the Navigator he and Manny were in.

"Are you sure he's dead?" Manny asked.

"Yeah, I'm sure he's dead. I told you I felt his neck and he had no pulse."

"And you said that the bracelet with the key to the safe on it was missing from his wrist, right?"

"Yeah, it was not on his wrist."

"So who the fuck has it?"

"Look around in the parking lot, there's a hundred of them to choose from."

"Do you think Perrish had anything to do with this at all?"

"Hell, no! That clever little bitch loved the ground Felipia walked on."

"Yeah, but for the right amount of money she would have had him killed or killed him herself."

"That's highly unlikely, besides she is the one that cleans his money up, so if she wanted everything she could have had it all a long time ago."

"I guess you're right, but I doubt the Moes had anything to do with this because even though they have been at war with us, their chief has a truce with The Devil who could have killed him on plenty of occasions. Felipia would have never come around here if he figured his life was in danger."

"Felipia was too cocky and arrogant as hell. He wouldn't have believed that another man on the face of the earth had the balls to assassinate him even if they had a gun pointed at the back of his head, and like you said, what good is truce between chiefs when a certain amount of money will make a man kill his own son?"

4

AFTER NOT HEARING FROM HER NEWPHEW who was supposed to have arrived by bus into Chicago four hours ago, Sandy picked up her cell phone and called his mother, her sister Portia, who was in New York.

"Hey baby. How are you?"

"I'm fine, so how's my baby boy?"

When her sister Sandy did not answer right away she knew that something was wrong.

"What happened, Sandy? Tell me," she said in a demanding voice that showed more concern then her sister wanted to hear.

"Well I just called his phone six times and he ain't answered yet. I even called the bus station and they said he got off and walked away from the station more than four hours ago."

"O my God," Portia said, sounding really worried.

Her son was in a city infested with gangsters and criminals who would kill you for wearing your hat on the wrong side.

"I'm coming down there!"

"No. No. Hold on a minute. I'm sure he'll call soon so don't start jumping to conclusions. I'm sure that he is ok."

"Well I will call his phone again, and if he doesn't answer this time I'll call the police and call you right back."

"Ok. Make sure you call me right back," Portia said, hanging up the phone.

Sandy looked around the room of her office and shook her head.

She had seen on the news that one of the crime bosses who ran one of the most ruthless gangs in Chicago had been murdered not far from where Denardo had gotten off the bus. But that wasn't unusual at all. She found his number pressed "send" on her cell phone and then listened as it began to ring.

"What's up, Aunt Sandy?" Denardo said, answering his phone after the first ring.

"Nigga!" Your silly sucka ass got me worried to death. I just got off the phone with your mother who is ready to jump on a plane and come down here looking for you herself.

"Where the hell are you?"

"I'm good, Auntie. I just met up with this girl and one thing lead to another," he said, watching Perrish as she made her way back towards the car.

"What the hell you mean with some girl? Your ass is down here to see me and I'm the only girl you need to be seeing right now, so make your way to the house or I'ma beat your ass, Denardo!"

"Ok. Ok, Auntie. I'ma make it home soon, just chill."

"Chill my ass! You got me all worried about you. I had to smoke two joints of weed out of my last bag of purple haze worried about your ass, and don't think you ain't gonna buy me another bag"

"Alright!" He said laughing, while watching Perrish and two huge men lift five duffle bags into the trunk.

She quickly dismissed the men saying something in Spanish that he couldn't understand, and the two men headed across the street while she made her way over to the driver's side door.

She opened the door and got inside, shutting it quickly to keep the disciples on the corner from looking inside.

"Did you get what you was looking for?" while ending the call.

"Yeah, I got it" she said, placing the black bag she was carrying between the seat.

"So who was you talking to?"

"That was my Aunt Sandy. She's worried sick about me and wondered why I didn't call her once I got to the city, that's all."

"How many people besides myself who are in Chicago actually know that you arrived here today and that you have an aunt that lives here as well?" She asked as she pulled from the side of the curb, heading down the street.

"No one," he said, scratching his head."

"Are you sure of that?" She replied sharply.

"Because these guys are gonna try to kill your aunt if and when they find out about you and her."

"I mean, I told this cab driver where I was going when he picked me up from in the middle of the street. At first he was pissed and he acted as if he really didn't wanna pick me up but he said he didn't mind taking me to the store after I paid him some extra money."

"Shit! Did this cab driver have any tattoos or was his hat cocked to the back?"

"Yeah, how did you know that?"

"Your aunt is in danger!"

"What do you mean my aunt is in danger?"

"Listen! All of the cabs work for the gangs in this city. How else do you think they get a pass to drop people off all over the city? They are the only ones that are allowed to cross boundaries to work, but in return for their safety passes they are informants for the gangs."

"What else did he say to you when you told him where you were going?"

"He acted scared like he couldn't drop me off at her building."

"That's because he's a Disciple,"

"Let me see this," snatching the phone out of his hand.

She dialed out, placing the phone to her ear and when the party on the other end answered,

"Listen! I need you to check on someone around there for me and do it now!"

"What's your aunt's address and building number?" she asked while turning her head to look at Denardo.

"Building 412, apartment 77,"

"You got that? Yeah, make sure nobody goes near that place and I mean nobody!"

"What the hell was that all about and who was that you were talking to?"

"That was my little brother and I'm trying to save your Aunt's life,"

"My aunt's at work, so what good is it gonna do to have somebody watching her place? Let me see the phone, I'ma call her and tell her to stay put until I get there."

He began dialing Sandy's number.

"Aunt Sandy, I'm on my way to pick you up so stay wherever you're at."

"I'm already on the fast train on my way home,"

"Look, I need you to stay away from your house for a while until I get there."

"Boy, you out of your gotdamned mind or something?"

"Naw, I got into it with some gangster up there at the store and somebody got hurt. I think they may know about you so just don't go home because your life may be in danger."

"Look here baby, a whole bunch of gangsters know about me and they know damned well not to come messing around with Sandy, that's WHAT THE HELL THEY

KNOW IF THEY KNOW WHAT'S GOOD FOR THEM! I been living in this city before Capone was running it and he couldn't run me out of my house so why in the hell am I supposed to be afraid of some BD's, GD's or ZZ?"

"Look man that's not the point; I just need you to hold up until I get there."

"Hold the hell on; let me check my mail box," placing the phone down as she used her key to open up the mail box."

"I thought you were just getting on the train?"

"I lied, now I'm inside my building about to head up to my apartment and ain't nobody around here gonna do a damned thing to me so stop all your worrying."

He looked at Perrish and shook his head.

"What's the matter?"

"She's already in her building and she's refusing to leave."

"That's good; at least we know that she's safe."

"How is she safe?" he asked with frustration.

"The Devil's Disciples won't have a chance of making it into Jeffrey Manor and making it out alive, so I guarantee you she's safe."

"Well what about us?"

"I'd rather go to one of my houses that not even The Devil knows about until we can figure all this out. Well what the hell are we waiting for?"

5

"ARE YOU SURE THIS CLOWN KNOWS WHAT HE'S TALKING ABOUT? Because if he doesn't, I'ma kill him right on the spot," Sleepy said with a frown."

"Didn't I just tell you that he told me he knows who did it?" Manny said, making his way pass the Cook County Jail.

When he reached the Popeye's he pulled to the side of the street allowing Sleepy to get out.

Sleepy made his way down the side walk heading toward the entrance of the Popeye's but before he could reach the door Caesar the Cab driver came walking out.

"So ya'll gonna take care of me right?" He asked as he walked up the side walk toward the truck

"Just get in the damn truck," Sleepy said, hopping into the back seat as Caesar slid over to the passenger side door and opened it. He climbed into the truck, closing the door behind him.

"So who did it?" Manny asked, turning his head to look at him.

"What about the money ya'll promised me?" Caesar asked, looking into the rear view mirror back at Sleepy.

"Didn't I tell you not to worry about getting paid? My fucking cousin just got assassinated and all you can think about is money?"

"You better tell us who the fuck did this before I kill your ass right here, right now," Sleepy said, putting his gun to the back of Caesar's head.

"Hold up! Calm down!" Manny interrupted.

"Caesar, we are gonna give you the fucking reward money, just tell us who did this first."

Caesar looked around at both of them, and then took a deep breath, letting it out.

"I picked this guy up from the bus station and he asked me to take him shopping which I figured was weird for 5 o'clock in the morning. The guy didn't even flinch when he seen all my tattoos. That's when I knew he wasn't from around the city. He asked me to take him around Jeffrey Manor where his aunt lives. Then I dropped him off at the store and he never came out of the door, so he had to be the one that killed The Devil."

Manny looked back at Sleepy whose jaw was clenched.

"Do you have the address of this aunt of this guy?"

Caesar grabbed a piece of paper and wrote down the building number and Sandy's apartment number, handing it over to Manny. Then he was ordered out of the truck.

"Go ahead and pay the man, Sleepy," Manny said, pulling away from the curb.

Sleepy fired two shots into the back of Caesar's head killing him instantly.

"You know we gonna have to call Little Devil and tell him about this?"

"Yeah, I know, Manny said. Why not just tell him that the Moes killed his dad so he can take them to war?"

"What good will that do?" Many asked.

"It'll give us enough time to locate Perrish and this guy and get the key to the safe from them."

"If the Little Devil gets to them first we can throw our chances of getting that money out the window."

"Yeah, and if we tell Little Devil that The Moes had something to do with his father's death, which he still doesn't know about, and he finds out that we are lying, what good is that money gonna do for us in our graves?" Manny asked.

"Knowing Lil Devil, he's gonna use the death of his father to take every one of the other gangs to war just to have reason to do it. We need to find Perrish and this mystery guy before they do. If she has the key then she is headed around Humble Park if she has not already been there. I say we go scope out the guy's aunt's place."

"Nigga, are you crazy? The Gangster disciples will kill us if they catch us anywhere near the Manor."

"I said scope it out, not go inside the building or near it."

"I know what we'll do. We are gonna call the twins and pay them to take care of this for us," Manny said smiling.

6

"WE SHOULDN'T EVEN BE IN THE CITY,"
Perrish said excitedly while making a left onto Damon.

"Aww, shit!" she said, looking into her rearview.

"What is it?" Denardo asked as he followed her
eyes.

He noticed the truck approaching them fast, which caused
Perrish to speed up. The truck carrying Manny and Sleepy
sped up as well, and once they were close enough to see
inside the driver's seat Sleepy rolled his window down and
told Perrish to pull over. She looked over at Denardo.

"Keep driving!" Denardo yelled, which caused her
to speed up.

"She's helping him," Manny said, slamming his fist
down on the dash board. "Kill them both!"

As they sped down the street, Sleepy opened fire, causing both Perrish and Denardo to duck low into theirs seats. "Unzip that bag on the back seat and you'll find some guns. Use them to get these assholes off us!" While she raced pass another car in front of her.

Denardo climbed into the back seat, grabbing hold of the bag and when he unzipped it he began to smile. He grabbed hold of a DDm4v7 assault rifle and two hand guns, climbing back in the front seat. Perrish grabbed one of the handguns and began firing backwards at Manny's truck making him swerve into a car. The impact from hitting the truck nearly caused Sleepy, who was hanging out the window, to fall from the car. Denardo pointed the Dm4 and opened fire. The bullets struck the front windshield of the car, its hood and the passenger side door.

"I'm hit, I'm hit!" Sleepy yelled as Manny raced past a car ahead of them.

Perrish made a sharp left onto Wolcott entering Killaward, which caused Manny who was in high pursuit of them to slow down.

"They're not following us anymore," Denardo said, looking behind them.

"We are now in Folk Turf, and no Spanish person is stupid enough to be caught dead around here."

"But you Spanish,"

"No. I'm black

"So who the hell was that shooting at us?"

"That was Manny and Sleepy, The Devil's younger cousins."

"How the hell did they find us that quick and why did they think that you are part of the death of their boss?"

"Well, you don't exactly have me at gunpoint now, do you? I told you your cab driver works for them so I guess he told them that we might be headed towards Jefferson Manor."

"I thought we were heading somewhere quiet to think first."

"Yeah we were, but since I was already so close to the Manor I figured I'd pick your Aunt Sandy up and take her with us."

"Thanks a lot, but you almost got us killed."

"Look who has the nerve to talk!" she said, batting her eyes at him.

"What in the hell is a Devil's Disciple anyway?"

"They're demons that live on earth amongst you and I, and their intentions are to bring hell to anyone that opposes them in any way. In order to be a Disciple you have to kill, its blood in and blood out with them. They don't believe in a God, and their God was the Devil and you killed him."

"Why the hell did you allow yourself to be involved with these types of people?"

"Everyone in Chicago is part of a gangster's life, either directly or indirectly and in a world where everything was so chaotic I tried my best to be an angel."

"You're an angel alright, The Devil's Angel."

"How dare you sit in my car after getting me into all this mess and try to judge me? She said, raising her voice. You're the one that ruined my life. I didn't barge into your life or stumble into your store at 5am talking about how much I believe that we were meant to be together, so don't dare try to judge me. And for your information, I wasn't involved with The Devil's Disciples; I was involved with The Devil himself."

"Yeah, and that makes all the difference."

They sat in silence until he noticed she was crying. He placed his hand on her shoulder.

"He wanted to marry me. He had grown tired of his son, he was having trouble controlling him, and so he told him that if anything was to happen to me he would let the Rule that was to go to him, go to Manny instead. By doing this he no longer had to worry about his son assassinating me or a child we might have had. When he told me what he did, I cried and told him I couldn't be with him after knowing about all the people he had killed or ordered to be killed."

"He gave me this," she said, holding her hand up to allow Denardo to get a closer look at the huge diamond on her ring finger.

"If you had no intention of marrying him, why the hell did you accept the ring?"

"Like every woman on the face of the earth, I wanted to believe he would change for me, for us, but he only got worse. He was trying so hard to eliminate all of his rivals so that he could abolish the five and six point start and bring everyone together under a seven point star or the seven point pitch fork. He felt that was the only way to acquire peace amongst the gangs." She said, dropping her eyes from Denardo.

"And?" replied Denardo

"I made him feel like there was still good in the world, even though he was apart of so much evil, and based on how he felt about me I could tell he was trying to change to be with me."

"'So were you gonna marry him if he eventually gave up that lifestyle and saw things your way?"

"I gave that question a lot of thought, but I knew that I never would be his wife. Felipia was possessed by the power he had, which made him think he was a God and I knew he wouldn't give that up for me or anybody else."

"You said that he loved you, but if he loved you so much why didn't he choose you over a lifestyle that was pushing you away from him?"

"I think it's like what happened to Saddam Hussein and Gaddafi. Both those men had so much to live for but they refuse to give up their position and live for everything else that mattered. Does that mean that they didn't love their possessions or their loved ones?"

"I think Felipia was like most every other man who promises himself to a woman."

"What do you mean by that?"

"I mean men get engaged to women in order to put them on lay-way plans. They enjoy the benefit of having a full-time lover, companion, friend and wife, but they themselves don't have to make a full commitment to that woman."

"It wasn't like that with us!"

"Look, Perrish, I'm not trying to be judgmental or anything but if he really wanted you like wanted you like most people want something. He would have done everything in his power to obtain you. He doesn't mind risking his life and the life of his Disciples to obtain his mission. He didn't mind killing and risking going to jail for his cause, but you mean to tell me that he wasn't willing to step away from all that to obtain what he believed was the reason the sun looked so perfect?"

"You think you've got this all figured out, don't you?" she said, throwing him a cute look.

"Naw, I don't have it all figured out, but I do know that if I have no problem making a decision whether to pay my bills or buy drugs, go into a woman without a condom, fight someone over something petty I'd let it go in a spilt second, it definitely doesn't take a year or better for me to decide if I like or love somebody enough to marry them."

"He would have married me if I let him. It was me who choose not to marry him. I told you, and the reason it took so long to decide was because I needed to see if he was really gonna change his life, I began to realize that he couldn't change for me or anymore else. In his world he was a Chief, a King, a Ruler of men, but in our world he was just a man who was in love."

"And that wasn't enough?"

Instead of answering him she remained quiet. They both just sat thinking to themselves as they came upon the outskirts of Chicago.

"Woman that allows herself to fall in love with a gangster or a thug is a fool, she said, wiping the tear that had fallen from her left eye onto her cheek. What security can you have loving someone who may be killed or locked up for life? How can you plan a future with a man whose past has already doomed his chances of seeing the future?"

Instead of answering her, Denardo just listened and she continued to cry and vent to him.

"I used to cry myself to sleep worrying about if he were dead or if he would be killed or jailed. Building a future with someone like that is like trying to build a paper house over a pit of fire. I was so foolish to believe that a nightmare would turn into a lovely dream one day."

"Trust me, I know what you went thought," he said, grabbing hold of her hand. He kissed it, placing it to his chest so that she could feel the rhythm of his heartbeat.

"Why did you say that you know what I'm going through?"

"Well, I had a similar relationship with a woman that I thought I loved and who I thought loved me. Dawn was beautiful, and I think only reason I fell for her was based on how she looked. In the end I came to understand

68

that I never even knew her, much less be able to say I loved her. Our relationship was based on desire, not feeling or careful thinking. She was attracted to me because I had money. When we had sex it was outstanding, but once the money was gone and I could no longer touch her, she realized that the reason she wanted me was gone so she left."

"What do you mean? When the money and the sex was gone?"

"I went to jail, so I couldn't provide for her the way she was used to, and I couldn't sex her the way that she was use to being sexed. She had an addiction to the male organ so she wanted something else to fulfill that addiction. She also started looking for another man to take care of her. Do I blame her? No. He said, shrugging his shoulders. She was in love with an illusion and when I went to jail she was forced to live out the reality behind that illusion."

"What did you go to jail for?"

"My mother's boyfriend beat her so bad that her face was unrecognizable. She went to the police but they didn't do anything but lock him up overnight. The next day I caught him beating her again, so I beat him within an inch of his life with his own gun. I don't regret it at all and if it happened again, I'd do it again because some things are worth dying and going to jail for."

"O my god, I'm so sorry!"

"I'm not."

"It wasn't like you went to jail for selling drugs or doing something she never knew you were involved with, so how can you not be mad that she left you and wasn't loyal enough to wait?"

"I never tricked myself into believing that a woman could handle jail when most men I know can't handle it. Being in prison is very hard on both people in the relationship and I never prepared her for what I was about to go through. I saw her when I got out. And she tried to get me back, but I couldn't go back to her after that. She cried, telling me that she wanted me; she just didn't want the situation. When two people choose to be together, their situations in life are no longer just theirs. I guess if I had cancer she would have left me saying she didn't want the situation," He said, cracking a smile that Perish could tell was not sincere. She could tell from the look in his eyes that what Dawn did to him was still bothering him.

His story about Dawn let her know that she really didn't love Felipia at all. He just happened to be there for her when no one else was there to help her. She reflected,

"Who would want to be caught courting her when a killer would be breathing down their necks?"

"Don't worry, when I told you that I loved you that I wanted to spend my entire life with you, I meant it,"

"How can you say you love me when you don't even know me or anything about me, for that matter?"

"I love the idea of what you represent. I know I would have no problem seeing your face next to me in bed for the rest of my life. I know that the feeling that came over me the first time I saw you was from my soul. I feel that when the Creator crafted all of us that you were made for me and I dreamed of you, so when I say that you are a dream come true, I tell you the truth."

His words made her want to cry. She pulled her car up to the gated community and let the window down, smiling at the security guard who sat in the booth.

"Hi Doctor Anderson," he said, opening up the gates to allow them to pass.

"Thank you," she said, making her way through the gate into the neighborhood in front of her.

On their way inside the neighborhood they passed two police patrol cars at the entrance of the well-to-do community.

"Who lives here?" he asked, looking over all the well decorated houses that seemed to have swimming pools and golf courses in the backyards.

"I do." She said, turning into the drive way of the largest house at the end of the long street.

"Wow! This is breath taking," he said, looking to his right at the beautifully manicured lawn behind the huge wooden fence surrounding her front yard.

When the door to the garage opened, she drove the car inside; he looked over to his right in amazement, beside him sat a pink McLaren.

To their left was a Porsche Cayenne truck.

"This is really nice,"

"I need a shower really bad," as she turned around walking over towards the door.

When she looked behind her and noticed that he wasn't following, she stopped, turning to look at him.

"What's wrong?"

"Is everything ok?"

Grabbing his hands while placing her head to his chest.

"My God, your hands are so sweaty and your heart is pounding like crazy!"

"I'm a little nervous, that's all,"

She could feel that he was trembling.

"All the stuff we been through today and not once were you nervous, but now that I got you alone, your trembling like a leaf." She said, kissing the back of his hand.

A tear fell from his eye as he looked down into her eyes. She stood up on her tippy toes and whispered in his ear,

"I promise not to hurt you."

Without really giving it any thought he reached down and palmed her butt, pulling her to him and without hesitation she wrapped her thighs around his waist and they began to kiss. He lifted her shirt, undoing her bra allowing her perky, soft, firm small breast to bounce forward. Her nipples, the color of red rust, instantly became hard which caused him to lower his head taking the right one into his mouth. As he caressed her nipple with his tongue and lips, she moaned while unzipping his pants.

She reached her hand down into his boxers and grabbed hold of his hard shaft, caressing it with her tiny soft fingers. He began kissing her neck while helping her remove his pants and once they were down to his feet he began to push her skirt back. He lifted it up and grabbed hold of her silky pink panties. With one hand he lifted her body up while with the other managed to remove her underwear, revealing the shaved diamond between her legs. Her organ was the most beautiful he had ever seen, The heat from her was warm and wanting which caused him to spread her lips apart with his hand as she guided him toward her. He caressed her tender softness while spreading her apart, and then slid himself inside her warm, wet, gentle inside, which nearly caused his knees to buckle. Looking down into her sparkling clear flawless grey eyes, he thrust himself inside her as far as he could, go, then pulled back, making her moan as she bit down into his neck. As he went back into her she could feel chills running down her spine, her whole body began to tingle. While palming her soft, voluptuous and luscious cheeks he could feel her thighs spreading further apart, giving him easy access to enter her further. As he pushed himself deeper inside of her she began to shake from the first orgasm she had ever had. Again the outer walls of her tenderly moist lips slid smoothly down on top of him, making him hold her even closer to him. Her organ was so tight; it was as if it had never been inhabited, which made him feel as if he and only he had been the only man to ever truly possess her. After going inside her gently, he thrust himself inside her with force which caused her to softly scream.

He continued to pound away at her inside as her juices allowed him to flow into her gently, and every stroke he made caused her to dig her nails deeper into his back as she bit down into his chest. The joy and pain she felt from feeling his erection inside her again caused her to have an orgasm. While she came, he continued to slide himself in and out of her honey mist. As she palmed the back of his head pulling him into her chest, he began sucking on her nipple again while stroking her with a constant motion he seemed to perfect. As he moved in and out she called his name in a soft, seductive way which made him spread her cheeks further apart in an effort to go inside her more deeply, as her tender vagina pulled tightly at him like a glove that fit perfectly. Together their bodies moved in a rhythmic motion. He turned her around, carrying her over to the front of the McLaren where he placed her down gently and eased her thighs apart even further.

"Yes, baby, Yes," she moaned, while watching him enter her with his massive and hard shaft.

He caressed her thighs and her skin, warm and silky soft to his touch. He pushed her thighs apart while caressing her skin and gently slid out of her, dropping down to his knees. He caressed her soft, moist lips with his hand while spreading her open. Then he placed his face between her thighs while touching her lips with his own. She palmed his head, leaning back on the car, and then closed her eyes while picturing his tongue upon her as he rolled back her clit and began to devour her pearl. She instantly began to come, moaning, which caused his hard shaft to feel as if it were about to explode.

He could feel her legs and her entire body shaking, but that didn't stop him from sucking her.

He looked up at her face, which showed she was feeling every inch of the passion he was applying with his lips, fingertips, hands and tongue. He watched, pleased to see that he was about to make her have another orgasm, and just as her moist eyes rolled back into her head, he sucked harder, pushing her thighs back upon the car's hood. As she moaned and tried her best to escape him, he continued to suck and she began to explode.

Without hesitating, he rose up between her thighs, grabbing hold of her, then flipped her over, raising her right leg up onto the car while spreading her cheeks apart. He then entered her, feeling the pleasure of the wet, warm juice inside. He interlocked his fingers with hers and stroked away until they both began to come. When he had climaxed, he laid his head upon her back, feeling the comfort of her butter-soft skin, while her warmth encompassed him, making him not want to move. She looked back at him with tears in her eyes and said,

"I guess you wanted to show me that you really do love me." This caused him to smile, and then he leaned down to kiss her.

He removed himself from inside her, using his shirt to wipe her clean. He held her in his arms as they slowly walked across the garage and up the steps into the house.

7

MORE THAN A BLOCK AND A HALF AWAY, Manny and Sleepy sat in Manny's Audi A8 and looking over toward Jeffrey Manor through night vision goggles.

"Where the hell are these two fools that you hired?" Sleepy asked in pain, grabbing his side where Denardo's two bullets had struck him.

"Are you sure you are ok?"

"Hell naw, I ain't ok, but I'm here now, so let's get this shit done before Little Devil ends up having us killed for what we are doing."

"I talked to De La Rosa and he told me that Little Devil already knows what's going on, so we gotta take care of this fast," Manny said lowering his goggles as he looked over at Sleepy.

"Did De la Rosa say if he knows what we were up to?"

"He's having some of his closet disciples handle Perrish's extension himself. From what I've heard, he's already destroyed every piece of property his father bought her and whatever else he knew about that was tied to her name. I'm quite sure he doesn't know about the boy who's with her or about his Aunt; he would have sent a team over here already."

"Good! He'll never know what Caesar told us because Caesar won't be talking to anyone else but the angels who question him in his grave," Sleepy said laughing but then he stopped because it hurt too much.

"I hope these Renegade Gangster Disciples can be trusted."

"As long as we pay them they can be trusted to do the job."

"I hope so, because from the looks of things the Gangsters got Jeffrey Manor on lockdown," he said, looking over at The Manor through his goggles.

"I see more than a thousand soldiers and there's no telling how many more of them there are inside the set."

"Are you sure that there's not a better way to do this without involving GD's?"

"These guys are tight. The only hope we have penetrating their ranks is through the renegades who pledge no allegiance to their king or chiefs. If we try to run up in their set we face instant annihilation."

8

IN THE BOTTOM OF AN EIGHTEEN-STORY BUILDING off California Avenue, into which no blacks were allowed to step foot, Little Devil sat on a Burgundy leather couch by himself. Two assault rifles rested nearby as he watched the huge 50-inch television screen in front of him. It showed Guerillas in Colombia battling the CIA. With the Winchester Carbine lying comfortably across his lap and the Barrington next to him, he sat calmly, without a worry in the world. Right in front of him on the table sat three things: A box of cigars stuffed with marijuana and ready to be smoked, two grenades and a 30-40 Krag assault rifle which was fully loaded. Two men who held rocket propelled Grenade launchers and their own assault rifles stood next to him on opposite ends of the couch. Little Devil, his entire body covered in tattoos, wore a white tank top and a pair of beige Armani slacks with black ACG Nike boots on his feet. A man wearing a perfectly cut Armani suit made his way over to the couch holding a black leather briefcase in his right hand. When he reached the couch he stopped and was quickly patted down by the man who stood at the end of the couch. He then was allowed to pass.

He walked over to the opposite side of the table in front of Little Devil and folded his arms, waiting for his Boss to give him permission to speak.

"Where are Manny and Sleepy?" Little Devil whose eyes were the color of blood asked, never taking his eyes off the television screen in front of him.

"We have not seen either of them since your father's assassination," the man said, looking down at the floor.

"Once you find them, kill them as well!"

Six-feet tall, solidly built Little Devil looked over at his men standing around the basement. He took the two assault rifles he had in both his hands and crossed them across his chest while throwing up a five-pointed star. Upon seeing this, his men began to toss up the two pistols they each carried along with the five pointed star.

This represented the seven-pointed star that was to abolish all the other stars, giving it ultimate rule over all the other gangs throughout America.

"Every sign of Perrish Hamilton's existence is to be wiped off the face of the earth," he said, flexing his chest.

He turned his head from side to side, looking over his men. They could see the huge tattoo under his neck which read "DISCIPLES".

"Once she is found and killed, bring her body to me so I can drink her blood", he said, raising his head to the ceiling.

9

THE INSIDE OF PERRISH'S HOUSE WAS LARGER THAN HE IMAGINED it would be from looking at it from the outside. The ceiling of the main level was twice as high as most homes, which reminded him of a gymnasium. He looked up at the golden chandelier hanging directly over his head in the middle of the living room. He then looked over the walls which were plastered with certificates she had received from her many accomplishments.

His attention was drawn to a silver plaque in the middle of the wall. He walked over to the wall to get a better look.

Enclosed in the frame was her doctor's certificate from American University Center.

Beside it was a gold medal from the Mayor of Chicago for her contributions to the city.

He studied the other certificates which caused him to smile, she was more important than he had figured.

"What are you looking at, baby?" She asked, while wrapping her arms around him from behind, then handing him a cup of hot tea.

He smiled and took the cup from her hand, sipping its content while turning around to face her. Seeing her caused his smile to grow even bigger. He kissed her on her lips then on her forehead, saying

"I didn't know you were a real doctor."

"Yes," she said, smiling as she looked over at her Ph.D Certificate in the stainless steel frame.

He looked her up and down and instantly became hard. She stood in front of him with the tea cup clutched between her fingers, wearing nothing but a white business shirt that barely covered her legs. Up under the see-through shirt he could see every detail of her body.

He placed the cup to the side and grabbed hold of her waist, kissing her.

"Your cocoa tasted much better than that tea," hearing this made Perrish smile.

"So what do you think about my house?" she asked, looking around at her self-decorated living room.

"It's very beautiful Perrish, but nothing will ever be as beautiful as you are to me."

What he said nearly brought her to tears, causing her to place her head on his chest.

"I wanna ask you something." He said, holding her tightly in his arms.

"I wanna know has The Devil or anybody else ever been inside this house?" The question caught her off guard, and she looked up into his eyes.

"No, I told you that we are safe! If anybody knew about this house I wouldn't have risked our lives bringing you here!"

"Did he pay for this place?" he asked looking away from her.

She pulled herself away from him with a frown, and then made her way across the floor, heading up a set of Mahogany steps leading in-between two Grandfather clocks and a huge redwood China cabinet.

Once she was standing there between the two grandfather clocks she stopped in her tracks, turning around to face him.

"You seem to think you know me so well. You should have known better than to ask me that question. A man doesn't make me. I make over $200,000 dollars a year being a Gynecologist, so your question was unnecessary, especially since you've just seen most of my accomplishments. That store in which you were in was also bought with my own money. So is this house and those cars you see out in my garage. I won't stand here and lie to you by saying that Felipia didn't give me things or spend money on me, but every house he bought for me and the cars he spent his money on are things I refused to accept."

Taking a deep breath she continued.

"I know that his son and his enemies alike know about the houses and cars, which means I'm a target for accepting those things. The only time I drove one of the cars or spent the night in one of the houses was when he was out of town. When I first met you I believed what you told me about us being together, because I always knew that God had someone besides Felipia out there for me. I had just given up thinking I would ever find him." She sighed, looking at Denardo.

"If you truly believe what you said to me then you should also believe that I will never put you in danger intentionally and that no man dead or alive could ever come between you and me," she said, shedding a tear,

Denardo crossed the floor and climbed the small set of steps over to her. He grabbed her, pulling her into his arms.

"I'm not worried about him; I'm worried about us,"

"You don't have to worry about anyone, I'm yours," she said kissing him.

"I just needed to know that we were safe in this house."

"I didn't get to be smart by being stupid. This house and all of my other properties I've worked hard for are in the names of politicians I can trust with my life."

"I love you," he said holding her tightly while breathing in her lovely scent.

10

MORE THAN THREE HUNDRED GANGSTER DISIPLES STOOD THROUGHOUT DENARDO'S AUNT'S BUILDING, making sure that nothing or no one went anywhere near where she stayed. As the fifteen heavily armed men in front of her apartment door stood steady, waiting on anything that appeared to be a threat to come about, Sandy stood in the middle of her living room floor with a open bottle of Patron in one hand and a smoking joint full of marijuana in the other. She danced to the sound of Al Greene's voice as it blared throughout her entire apartment from the huge surround sound system she had hooked up throughout the entire place.

As if she didn't have a worry in the world, she placed the bottle to her lips and guzzled down the strong liquor without flinching from its harsh taste, which burned her throat as it went down. She chased the liquor down with a cloud of smoke which she then blew out after nearly coughing up one of her lungs.

She sat the bottle down on the table next to her and patted her chest with her free hand. She then made her way over to the front door, looking out the peep hole into the hallway.

After shaking her head upon seeing The Disciples all spread-out throughout the hallway she said,

"These niggas got me fucked up; I ain't no punk bitch by far!" She left the door and walked back to the table to retrieve the half empty bottle of Patron.

She grabbed the bottle and spun around, while doing a two-step. She continued to dance as she was very careful not to stagger too far with her intoxication.

Across the street from her building on the thirteenth floor, Perrish's brother, M-Jettic, stood beside Rio, the GD's Chief. He turned to the old man and said,

"My sister is trippin, no fool in his right mind gonna try to storm up in this hood trying nothing!"

"Do you question your sister's judgment or do you question mine?" Rio asked, turning to face him.

"You should have let me deal with this the way I had intended to deal with it, that's all. We was fine with Poppy Luie, Diggar and Kequan on her door. All them other Disciples can be on another mission right now, that's all," he said, shrugging his shoulders.

"See, that's why some people are princes and some are chiefs," Rio said, looking down into the parking lot that sat in the middle of all the buildings.

11

"**WHERE THE HELL ARE THESE TWO IDIOTS?**" Sleepy said, looking over at Manny, still with the goggles up to his eyes. He was peering over into Jeffrey Manor.

Before Manny could put down the goggles and answer him, the back door opened and a jet-black man with dred locs, grey eyes, wearing a black hoodie jumped into the back seat.

"What the fuck, you almost got yourself shot!" the startled Sleepy said, turning around to face him with a look of disappointment.

"Me Brudda don't take kind to threats, so watch your tongue," Screw blood said, removing the hoodie.

Again Sleepy was startled. Screw blood's identical twin Maniac Seville stood at the passenger side window with an AK-47 assault rifle pointed down at him.

"Me got four ears so me hear every ting." Screw Blood said, removing the Calico fully-automatic pistol from his waistline placing it down onto his lap.

"Ok, let's get down to business," Manny said, handing him a piece of paper.

"All dey numbers not correct," Screw Blood said, looking up at Manny.

"That address has to be her address," Manny said, frustrated.

"I'm not speaking about she address; I'm speaking about me money dred!"

"Shit! Twenty thousand per head is more than anybody gets paid to kill," Sleepy said, raising his voice.

Maniac Seville placed a red beam attached to his weapon on Sleepy's forehead.

"Calm down! Everybody just calm down," Manny said, looking into Screw Bloods dark, mysterious grey eyes.

"How much is it that you are asking for?"

"A step to a ladder," Screw Blood said, smiling.

Sleepy shook his head, wanting to say something, but he was sure that Maniac Seville (known as a ghost, but said to have killed over a hundred people) would fire on him as soon as he did, so he just shook his head and remained quiet.

Manny reached over Sleepy and opened the glove box, which contained stacks of money. He grabbed two of the stacks and handed them back to Screw Blood who flipped through them, then placed it in his hoodie pouch.

"Me and me brudda gone have to kill up a bunch of men for this money."

"So what! That's what ya'll do anyways," said Sleepy.

"Even though I be Renegade, me don't like killing me own Gangster Disciples," Screw Blood said pointing the Calico at Sleepy's chest.

"Men like you two I would kill for free, but I hate to kill the gangsters unless the money is right," he said, grabbing hold of the door knob and stepping out of the car. Before he could open the door all the way Sleepy looked toward his window and Maniac Seville was gone.

He and Manny looked around for the man but saw no sign of him, as if he hadn't been there at all.

They watched as Screw Blood made his way up the block and across the street into The Manor.

"I can't believe you gave that punk a whole hundred grand," Sleepy said, nodding his head as he looked out his window to make sure Maniac Seville wasn't listening.

"Don't worry about the money. It's a highly unlikely chance that either of them will live to spend it anyways. They'll never make it out of The Manor alive."

12

MANIAC SEVILLE STOPPED IN THE WOODS TO GATHER A MP5 ASSAULT RIFLE HE HAD STASHED, and a bag of other weapons which included over ten hand grenades. He then walked cautiously around to Sandy's building from the back, without being seen by the thirty GD's waiting at the building's back side. He slipped up the catwalk, climbing up to the eighth floor.

As his brother made his way inside the building, Screw Blood traveled through the crowd of GD's stationed in front of the building. He was greeted, and with his hand raised low he returned the greeting while continuing to make his way towards the entrance of her building.

He reached the front steps where over a hundred GD's hung out and continued forward until he was up the steps and inside the building.

Again he gave the greeting to the men in the hallway as he walked over to the steps. He entered the stairwell and quickly traveled up to the eighth floor. His brother was waiting at the end of the dark hallway with his weapons pointed at the fifteen GD's standing guard outside Sandy's apartment.

Screw Blood made his way off the stairwell onto the 8th floor, down the hallway toward Sandy's apartment as fifteen stone-faced gangsters watched his every move.

When he reached the men, the hugest of them stepped out from the crowd and put his hand into Screw's chest, stopping him, making Screw give him a funny look.

"Nobody goes down this hallway for nothing," and that's the Chief's orders," the man said with a frown.

Maniac Seville knew that his brother was in trouble. He pulled two flash bang grenades out of the bag between his feet.

He pulled the pin, rolling both the grenades down the hallway toward the men who were prepared to attack Screw Blood if he went any further.

"Fuck your Chief!" Screw Blood said, pulling his weapon while diving to the ground.

As soon as he did, the flash grenades blew up, crushing more than seven of the GD's and killing them instantly. Maniac Seville then opened up two assault rifles, killing the rest of them.

Upon hearing the explosions and the gun fire, the GD's throughout the whole building ran toward the eighth floor. Sandy ran down the hall. She hid inside the hallway closet.

Screw Blood made it to his feet and at a running pace he charged the door, kicking it in with force. The door struck the wall, making a huge banging sound, which made Sandy, already crying, cover her mouth. He waved the Calico back and forth while scanning the entire apartment very carefully. He checked the kitchen cabinets and when he didn't see any sign of her he made his way down the hall. When he reached the hallway closet he stopped and turned to face it. Sandy tried her best not to make a sound, but her sniffling was louder than she had expected, which caused him to open the door. He found her sitting in a fetal position, which made him smile. The closet was dark, so he never saw the small caliber pistol she held until he stepped into the closet and heard the startling sound of six tiny pops.

Two of her bullets grazed him, making him raise his weapon and pull the trigger. He fired the high-powered automatic pistol more than thirty-two times and more than twenty-seven bullets hit Sandy's small frame, tearing it to shreds. He grabbed his shoulder checking to see how badly he was hit, but when he heard the sound of the multiple caliber weapons being fired, concern for his brother's safety caused him to rush back towards the door. He peeped out and saw bullets flying back and forth down the hallway. He knew there was no way he was going to make it out of the apartment without being hit.

Just then he heard a loud explosion and the gunfire ceased for awhile. He then hears Maniac calling his name making him bolt from the apartment and head down the hallway toward where his brother stood waiting for him.

Maniac continued to fire down the hall cautiously to make sure he didn't hit Screw Blood. Once they were back together, they ran towards the fire escape at the back of the building, which was now empty. All the men who had been standing guard ran into the building which gave the brothers a clear path to make their escape.

13

AS HE WAITED ON PERRISH TO RETURN, Denardo sat in the bed naked, smiling to himself, while looking up at the ceiling thinking about how blessed he was to have found his true love in the midst of so much chaos. Thoughts of how to escape the city began to run through his head.

"Damn! I got it!" he said, throwing the comforter off as he jumped out of bed.

He grabbed his jeans off the floor, slipping them on as he raced across the huge room and out the door.

He traveled down the hallway until he reached the stairwell, descending with speed.

In no time he was on the main level of the house looking for Perrish. While smiling, he called to her and when she didn't answer he became worried. He walked around throughout the house looking for her and when he reached the kitchen he saw her in the corner near the pantry sitting in the fetal position with her head in her knees.

"Baby! I got it! I know exactly how we can get out of the city and how we can get my Aunt Sandy out of The Manor safely," he said, moving quickly over to her.

He stood over her and called out her name. When she raised her head he seen that she had been crying.

"What's wrong?"

He grabbed hold of her hands and smiled, saying

"I know how we can leave here without any more problems."

A tear fell from her eyes and she shook her head, sobbing,

"I'm so so sorry."

"Sorry for what? We can leave now!"

"No! We can't leave now," she said placing her hands up to his face.

"What are you talking about? You promised to leave with me."

She kissed him on his forehead looking into his eyes, then said,

"Aunt Sandy was murdered."

The news of Sandy's death hit him like a ton of bricks. He felt his chest getting tight for some reason he could barely breathe. As he began to cry Perrish pulled him to her chest and held him. She whispered in his ear.

"They all will die for this, I promise. **THEY ALL ARE GONNA GO STRAIGHT TO HELL AFTER I KILL THEM!"**

14

"HAS EVERYTHING THAT SHE OWNS BEEN BURNED?" A blood shot-eyed Little Devil asked as he stood on the pier out on the great lake.

He looked out into the water that flowed slowly in front of him.

"Absolutely! We've destroyed everything that bitch owns except the hospital where she works," said a man whose entire face was covered in gang graffiti.

He stood behind his Chief.

"Go to the hospital and find her, I want her put in the ground before the sunrises over this body of water tomorrow," Little Devil said, turning to face the man.

"Make sure we have someone watching the trains, buses and airports. If that bitch gets out of this city then you take her place on the cutting block!"

15

ON THE ROOF OF THE CHICAGO MEMORIAL HOSPITAL, Denardo sat watching the parking lot through the scope of a Remington 700.

"I don't see any sign of the Disciples, but there is a suspicious car to your right that three men have been sitting inside all day," he said, speaking into his walkie-talkie. Perrish on the other end was disguised as a man inside of a blue tinted-window station wagon in the hospital parking lot.

"I'ma go now," she said, grabbing hold of the door knob.

She stepped outside the car and headed straight for the front of the hospital as he watched her every move, making sure no one dared to approach. He watched as the men in the car sat watching the parking lot still. The disguise had worked but even disguised as a man she looked gorgeous,

Denardo thought to himself. Once she was inside the hospital she made her way over to the elevator traveling up to the thirteenth floor.

When the door opened she stepped out and traveled down the hallway to a huge black door. She had to use her key card and punch in a code to unlock it. Once inside, she locked the door, crossing softly across the floor. She used a key on her key ring to open up two huge yellow file cabinets that were full of medicine and flammable liquids. She quickly packed bottles in a bag, and once it was full she pulled out another bag, filling that one as well. Just as she finished filling the second bag, a piece of the drop ceiling above her head was removed and Denardo descended down into the room from a rope. Perrish stopped what she was doing and began hugging and kissing him. He then scooped up the bags and used the access rope to pull them up into the ceiling one by one.

Before he climbed back into the ceiling he turned, looking into her eyes which made her place her head on his chest. She told him to be careful. He then kissed her forehead, grabbed hold of the rope and raised himself back into the roof, placing the drop ceiling over the hole he had descended from. She quickly began taking the baggy clothes off and once she was out of them, she stashed them, moving back out into the hallway.

She traveled down toward the end of the hall and made a left, heading into the Children's Center.

"Your patient has already arrived and I have her dressed and ready for her exam." the gorgeous brown-skinned woman sitting across the office at her desk said, looking up at Perrish.

"Thank you, Nurse Anderson," Perrish said, smiling.

She made her way over to an empty computer, typed something in, and then waited for it to print out. Once the copy had printed, she snatched it up and headed into another room where a beautiful little girl no older than eight years old sat on the table in a paper night gown.

"Mommy," the little girl Ayana said, holding her arms open wide, waiting for Perrish to hug her.

Perrish made her way across the room and hugged her, and for a long time while they just held each other.

"Ayana, I want you to know that your father was killed by some bad men the other day and now you are gonna have to stay with your brother Felipia Junior."

"No! No! I don't wanna stay with him! I want you, mommy! I want you!" she said crying.

Perrish pulled out her cell phone and began recording Ayana crying. She turned the camera to her right where Ayana's underwear and clothes lay spread out on a table. She recorded the articles of clothes then shut the camera off, hugging Ayana.

"Don't worry, I'll never allow anything to happen to you," Perrish said, hugging her tightly.

She then slipped her hand inside her white doctor's coat and pulled out a small brown bottle which she opened carefully. She poured some of the liquid out of the bottle onto a small rag and held it over Ayana's face until she closed her eyes and went to sleep. Perrish laid her back on the bed and grabbed a wheelchair. Then made her way out of the room with her.

In order to keep from being seen, she used the stairwell. When she and Ayana reached the first floor, she headed straight for the exit next to the major trauma ward.

As the door opened for her to leave, two officers carried in four men who had been badly burned. A Disciple tattoo on one of the men's inner palm caused Perrish to stop in her tracks.

"Officer, what is wrong with these men?" she asked.

"They were shot up pretty bad and if they aren't seen by a doctor as soon as possible, we doubt any of them will make it."

Perrish, realizing she should have stuck to her plan and left, but instead turned Ayana around and told the officer to bring the man, leading him into the major trauma unit.

She placed Ayana where she could see her, then slipped on a gown doctors used to operate on patients. She slipped on a pair of latex gloves, ordering the two officers to lift the man up on the counter. Once they did, she ordered them to leave. One of the officers handcuffed the man, saying

"He was involved in a shooting that left three other people dead, so I have to cuff him."

"I'll be fine, just go stand outside the door," Perrish said, pulling the curtain in front of her to separate her from the officer.

He took the hint and went to join his partner standing guard outside the door.

After tearing open the man's shirt to see if he was still alive, Perrish reached into her pocket, retrieving another small vial of liquid. She grabbed a syringe off the table beside her and stuck it into the bottle, drawing up the liquid whose label read Sodium Thiopental, which to most was known as Truth Serum. She stuck the needle into the man's chest right over his heart and waited. The man opened his eyes slightly and began to moan.

"Where is Felipia Junior?" she asked, leaning closer to his head in order to hear him.

In a whisper the man gave her the location of the warehouse off of California Avenue where Little Devil had been last time he had seen him.

"Where else would he be?"

"He is expected to hold a meeting with his top Disciples about demolishing the five and six-point star tonight."

"Where?" she asked, raising her voice.

"At the Devil's Layer"

"What happened to you?"

"Little Devil has started a war with all the other sets we were ambushed," he said, closing his eyes.

She checked his pulse but felt nothing. Quickly she made her way over to Ayana, grabbing the wheelchair she sat in. She then made her way out of the hospital and as she did, Denardo fired a single shot into the gas tank of the Assassins car blowing it up. While everyone in the hospital panicked and ran to see what had happened; Perrish left the building made it back to the station wagon, placing Ayana inside, and drove off undetected.

16

"I NEED TO GET EVERYTHING DONE BEFORE I LEAVE FOR HAWAII TOMORROW NIGHT," Rio said.

He was sitting in the back of a bulletproof black-on-black Maybach between two of his body guards looking down at his schedule on his phone's screen.

The nine-car entourage with his car in the middle made a right and continued straight down a street that the Gangster Disciples had completely shut down, allowing him to travel in safety.

He looked out his window and was amazed to see that he, one man, had enough power to shut down every street he passed by each and every time he moved from one place to another.

"Damn! What's taking so long?" he asked, looking down at the diamond emblazoned Rolex that sat high upon his wrist.

"We should be pulling up to the spot in less than five," the huge man next to him said. He was sitting with a semi-automatic shotgun in his hands, peering through his dark shades at his Chief.

"Where is my son?" Rio asked, placing his phone to his ear.

"He's in the car second from the last," the man sitting to his right answered.

"I hope this damned meeting isn't drawn out, because I have to pack for my trip

"What the hell?" Rio said, nearly falling into the laps of his bodyguards. The car he was in swerved left, then right all in almost one motion.

Before the driver could straighten the vehicle out, three dump trucks were coming at them full speed and side swiped the car, sending it over the railing and down the adjacent grass hill.

The entourage of cars behind him were also caught up in the impact of the huge trucks that side-swiped them.

More than forty men emerged from the back of the three dump trucks and opened fire on the cars with automatic weapons. Neither Rio nor any of his men had a chance of surviving. Those that hadn't been instantly killed from the impact of the crash died from the assault in which over 5,000 bullets were fired into their vehicles. When the men stopped firing, all that was left of the cars were bullet-riddled pieces of metal.

17

THE ASSASSINATION OF RIO HAD THE GD'S ON HIGH ALERT and everyone they had beef with was now at risk of being fired on. The Chiefs in the other gangs began to fear for their lives because without their own chief, nearly all of the GD's had taken up the position of a renegade, meaning that nobody nowhere was safe in the streets of Chicago.

M-Jettic, now acting Chief of the Gangster Disciples, ordered his men to kill any and everyone they felt was responsible for the death of their Chief. The streets of Chicago had become a war zone which was exactly what Little Devil wanted.

Once he had succeeded at turning the gangs against each other and eliminating their Chiefs, Little Devil knew that allegiance to the five and six point star would no longer mean anything to anyone, giving him the opportunity to enforce the seven-point star.

Seventeen year-old Saboor Shareef, who spoke Spanish and looked as if he were of Spanish descent (but was really African -American mixed with Moroccan) drove his black Bronco up California Avenue. He continued to drive until he was deep into the heart of what was known as "The Village."

The gangsters who thought that he was Spanish allowed him to get out of the car and make his way through the crowd over toward the middle building, as he had done so many other times, but this time was different. Shareef walked toward the alley, unzipped his coat, grabbing hold of the trigger that was designed to set off the forty pounds of plastic explosives in the trunk of his truck. He continued to walk nervously and once he reached the end of the alley where a mob of over sixty men stood congregating, he pushed the button.

The impact of the explosion tore through The Village, nearly leveling two of the eighteen-story buildings. Debris, ash and pieces of bricks went flying in every direction killing most of the people who had been standing around outside.

As the ground under his feet shook, Shareef watched as the men, all in a state of panic, ran toward him, trying to make it over to what was left of the buildings.

He waited until most of the men who were running at full speed passed him, and then he reached into his jacket pulling out two M2-40Bravo assault rifles equipped with over a hundred rounds. He pointed the weapons and opened fire on the men, chopping them down like a lawnmower on blades of wet grass.

He then set off the bomb vest he had strapped to his body which blew him to shreds and leveled the eighteen-story building he stood beside.

When the dust settled in The Village, more than thirty people had been killed and hundreds more had life-threatening injuries.

18

THE SPIKE IN VIOLENCE AND THE EMPLOYMENT OF TALIBAN AL-QAEDA TYPE guerilla attacks the gangs were using to take each other out had caught the eye of the President, creating a political firestorm. This caused congress to put pressure on the Director of the Federal Bureau of Investigation and Homeland Security to crack down on every gangster living within the city of Chicago.

Agent Rumsfeld, the Director of Homeland Security, made his way down the long hallway of the FBI headquarters in Washington, D.C.

He swung the black briefcase gripped tightly in his right hand as he nervously walked down the hall leading to the conference room. Once he reached the conference room, Secret Service held the door open for him, allowing him to walk into the huge office where over two hundred

Homeland Security agents and a hundred or so FBI agents sat waiting for him to address them. He approached the podium set up at the front of the room, all eyes on him.

Once he reached the podium he rests the briefcase on top and opened it while clearing his throat. Staring out over the faces of the roomful of agents he again became nervous until he saw Congresswoman Betty Ford sitting in the back of the room beside Congressman Levi.

Rumsfeld loosened his tie and adjusted the microphone so that it was directly in front of his mouth.

"Ladies and gentlemen, we have what I would like to call a high alert. We have local gangs and petty gangsters employing Afghanistan type terrorist attacks on each other. The President of the United States has personally called me and told me this must be dealt with immediately. These men are lawless, so trying to make sure that their Constitutional rights are protected will be a waste of our time. In order to stop these Villains I am giving you permission to use any force necessary."

Nearly every hand in the room went up, and after looking over to many curious faces in the room, he rested his eyes upon the most pleasant one; A brunette with green eyes. He pointed his finger at her and she lowered her hand and began to speak.

"Sir, with all due respect, if we are really going to take these petty thugs seriously like modern Al Capone or something, and say we do put an end to the rise in violence that has been occurring throughout the streets of Chicago. Do you really think we can stomp out the existence of gangs which are embedded into the fabric of our society?"

After rubbing his chin a few times, Rumsfeld looked her square in the eyes and said,

"Al Capone never blew up or leveled two buildings in a crowded neighborhood."

"No organized crime syndicate has killed more men in the streets of our cities than these gangs have. We are not dealing with petty criminals. We are dealing with killers who will hurt, murder, rob and rape anyone they damned well please, and quite frankly I believe these men are more deadly than Bin Laden or Saddam Hussein. These men are bold enough to commit their crimes in the heartland of our country, which is more than I can say for most terrorists who have yet to succeed in doing so."

He stepped down from the podium, making his way toward the group which had begun to stand.

He made his way over to the middle of the room where he was completely surrounded. He then said,

"I want these men and their lifestyle put to an end! I don't give a damn how you men and women have to do it as long as it gets done. If Colombian or Mexican Cartels are doing business with them, start rounding them up as well. I want to hit these people where it hurts, even if that means indicting their mothers and grandmothers for looking after the bastards in their childhoods. As of right now the city of Chicago is under siege by the government of the United States. No one is going into the city and no one is allowed to travel outside of it without first being given permission by me."

19

OFF OF BURNS SIDE STREET MORE THAN TWO HUNDRED BLACK PEACE STONE'S in all black gave gang signs with their hands while saying "All's Well" to the group of four men coming toward them. The four men returned the greeting with a smile as they continued to make their way into the Heavily-Black-Stone infested and controlled projects. Again the men who had come upon another group of Stones were greeted and instead of saying anything, they held their fists to their chests, spreading all five fingers apart to indicate they were Stones or riding up under the five-point star.

The group of men that occupied the entire curb parted to allow them to pass, and just as they all were past and the heavy crowd occupying the parking lot in the middle of the projects, they pulled their coats open, revealing collapsible stocked M4 assault rifles and began spraying into the crowd.

People screamed, trying to run for cover and were chopped down by gunfire. The four men made their way deeper into the Stone-infested neighborhood as if they had a wish to die.

With every step they continued to spray bullets until met by a force they themselves could not repel. More than two hundred Stones emerged from the buildings, firing assault rifles and pistols at the men. After nearly an hour stand-off the four men lay dead.

The Stones stood around in a state of disbelief, not understanding how somebody could be so bold as to assault them deep in the heart of their own turf.

Although everybody had an opinion, nobody said a thing but war was the thought on every one of the angry men's minds.

20

TRUMAN PROJECTS, OR HOLY LAND AS IT WAS KNOWN TO THE CITY OF CHICAGO and to the Vice Lords who considered it the birth place of their crown, was considered to be a place that not even the police could come into without having a problem getting out. And with all the violence that was jumping off with all the other gangs, the security in and around Truman was as heavy as it had ever been, making anyone who dared to consider assaulting the Lords there think twice.

Basically, for anyone to get inside of Truman they had to be on a suicide mission with no intent of making it out of Truman alive. On each side of the street that led up into Truman, Lords stood on every inch of the sidewalk. Any and every truck or car that made it up the driveway into Truman was being scrutinized heavily by the Lords.

Mr. Phil, as he was known to the Vice Lords, drove his school bus (converted into a seafood and fried chicken restaurant) into Truman. When the Lords saw him they allowed him to pass without holding him up. He drove his truck into the middle of the circle and rang the ice cream truck bell to get his loyal customers attention.

Before he could cut the alarm off a crowd of adults and kids gathered around the front and side of the truck in hopes of getting a plate of the old man's famous chicken.

Mr. Phil whose entire family lived inside of Truman and who were like he was, all Vice Lord, were the only ones that didn't make their way to the truck. But why would they? When they got all the fried chicken they wanted whenever they wanted?

The crowd gathering around the truck seemed to get larger and larger; Mr. Phil approached the window and opened it.

"Ay, Mr. Phil, give me some of that good chicken," one of the men said, smiling as he fumbles through a knot full of money in his hands.

Mr. Phil looked out over the faces of the beautiful children, women and men and began to cry.

"I'm sorry," he said, reaching over to his cash register. He flipped a red button at the bottom of the cash drawer and the entire truck exploded.

Little Devil, watching the entire thing from his Television, laughed hysterically.

"Boss, should I let his family go now?"

The man standing next to him asked which caused Little Devil to look up at him with a smirk on his face.

"Kill them as well," he said, turning his head from the man.

21

AS THE SIX BRAND-NEW C1500 SILVER MERCEDES BENZES MADE THEIR WAY UP 69TH STREET, an entourage of GD's heading in the opposite direction made a sharp U-turn and began trailing behind them.

"That's them, that's that nigga Little Devil and his Disciples," Smuddy, the GD's Prince said to the entourage of men watching with him in the truck.

His driver picked up his Nextel phone and alerted the other four trucks full of Gangsters to be prepared. They followed the cars as they drove up into Inglewood, one of the GD's strongholds.

"These mutha fuckers think they slick. They're about to go shoot up the hood in new cars thinking nobody will be expecting it," Smuddy said, fuming with anger in the back seat.

They continued to follow the Mercedes until they pulled to the side of the road.

"What the hell are they stopping for?" Asked the man driving the first truck, slowly approaching the last vehicle in the line of cars.

"Yo boss, what should we do?" He asked while radioing to Smuddy.

"Unleash hell and spare none of them!" He yelled into the phone loud enough for all the other GDs to hear.

As the men began to step out of the cars, all four of the trucks sped up to them. The GDs hopped out of the truck with their weapons drawn and began to open fire on the men.

After taking shelter behind their vehicles, the men whom Smuddy had assumed were Devil's Disciples (or some other hostile gangsters coming to attack them) returned fire. As they did the GD's fired back. Men stood on both sides of the street and in the middle of it firing high power assault rifles as if they didn't have a care in the world.

Smuddy kneeled down and took aim at one of the men, then fired his weapon, striking the man in the head.

As his lifeless body fell to the ground, Smuddy watched with a smile on his face. It wasn't until the man hit the ground and his jacket opened, revealing the gold-colored FBI badge that Smuddy's entire facial expression changed.

"Stop! Stop!" He screamed, trying to get the attention of his men, but with all of the gunshots ringing off his words was muffled.

He jumped across into the driver's seat, put the truck in drive, and then sped off, leaving his men taking shelter behind the truck to be hit by oncoming gunfire. As he sped away, one of the federal agents fired several shots at the truck but he was gunned down as well.

As he drove he began to see flashing lights headed up the street in the direction he was driving, causing him to step on the brakes. More than forty cars were headed in his direction. He looked behind at the small war that was still ragging on and he then began to see that even more police cars were coming from the back to block the street off.

"Shit! Shit! Shit!" He screamed, slamming his fist down onto the steering wheel, frustrated.

He knew that he was done running and there was no way to escape. He took the car out of park and stepped on the gas, flying down toward the roadblock and as he got in reach of them, the police started firing at the truck. The truck struck the first car, knocking it out of the way but when it reached the second car it flipped over, landing on its side. All the officers and agents who held their guns waiting to see if anyone got out of the car continued to watch well alert.

Smuddy, who grabbed hold of an assault rifle, slide out the window and across the ground on his back. He tried to stand but was shot. He opened fire but was gunned down before he could do any damage to anyone.

For a while the GDs in his entourage held the feds off but after two hours of back-to-back gunfire, all fifteen of the GDs lay dead in the street around their bullet-ridden vehicles, and two of the federal agents lay dead with over five of them seriously wounded.

The death of the federal agents who the news claimed were hunted down like animals and killed in the streets gang style, drove Director of the FBI Agent Fisher and Agent Mathew, in charge of Homeland's Security's City under Siege movement both mad. Together they headed into the Capital to speak to Holdem, The United States Attorney General.

They made their way up the long set of steps leading up to the Capital, and after being checked through several security check points along the way, were finally standing outside the Attorney General's Office.

"He's waiting to see you," a gorgeous Brunette said.

She wore a miniskirt so tight that nearly nothing was left to the imagination. As she led them into the Attorney General's office, both men admired how her very shapely booty jumped around within the tight fabric that concealed it. Both men felt themselves getting hard as they continued to admire her sexy strut.

"Here we are," she said, turning to face them with a smile while flipping her long ponytail behind her.

Both men looked into her misty blue eyes, intrigued at how attractive she was.

"Thank you," Agent Mathew said, making his way past her into the huge office.

Agent Fisher just stood looking down at the diamond shape between her legs. She smiled then said,

"They're waiting on you sir."

"O yeah, I'm sorry." He said, walking pass her so closely he could feel the heat from her body while inhaling a whiff of her perfume.

She closed the door and strutted off in the same direction she had come from.

"Angel has that effect on all men," Holdem said, standing up from his desk.

He extended his hand to Marshal who was the first to embrace him.

"Have a seat." He said, pointing to the two huge brown leather chairs in front of his desk.

Both men sat down, crossing their legs in different directions.

"So I hear you have a serious problem," Holdem said, grabbing a cigar from his desk and placing it into his mouth.

"Ay, yes, we have a bunch of problems," Agent Marshal said, pulling the small black briefcase he had carried with him into his lap.

He unzipped it, pulling out a stack of documents which he began to put upon the Attorney General's desk.

"Hold them, there's no need," the Attorney General said, waving him off while lighting the cigar hanging from his lips.

He blew a huge cloud of smoke toward the men as they watched it waft toward them.

"These things will kill you," he said, smiling as he removed the cigar from his mouth.

"Now exactly what is it that I can help you boys with?" He asked, placing the cigar back into his mouth.

"Sir, we have a problem that has escalated to the gangsters who are attacking and killing our Agents."

"See, that's the problem," the Attorney General said, blowing another cloud of smoke from his cigar into the air above his head.

"You fellas are dealing with killers who won't hesitate to kill you or their own mothers. You have to become killers instead of lawmen in order to control these beasts. You see, we had a problem with the Mafia once, a bunch of Italians who thought they could run our country for us by using violence and fear."

"We found out why so many people were scared to death to cross these guys, and once we found out why, we began installing a hundred times worse fear into these gangsters. All the Mafia could do was kill them or their families but We; The Government of the United States could keep them alive and make them all wish that they had been killed. Now we have mob bosses even snitching and begging us to protect them!"

"So let me get this straight, you want us to become even more violent than the men we are after?"

"Exactly!" Holdem said, and smiled while spreading his arms.

Mathew looked over at Fisher who shrugged his shoulders.

"You know why Mob bosses come to us to protect them?"

Both men remained silent, shrugging their shoulders.

"It's because we can not only kill them, we can take every damned thing they worked for, lock them in a tiny dirty cell, take their family from them and make them wish everyday they were dead."

"Once you can conquer a man's fear, you take that fear that he once had and multiply it times the amount of miles it takes to get up to the sun. Now go turn the heat up on them sons of bitches and remember that you are licensed to kill, and once you do you'll even get a medal for it. Fire must be fought with an even greater form of fire."

"Now if you gentlemen will excuse me, I have a hot date," he said, yelling out for Angel, who reappeared out of nowhere.

Both men got to their feet and made their way out of the Attorney General's office, but not before turning to take a last peek at the gorgeous brunette standing with her legs crossed up against the Attorney General's desk.

Once they were outside his office and back in the hallway, Fisher turned to Mathew and said,

"This freaking guy is crazy as a tick on an iron dog."

"I know, and that's why he's the Attorney General."

"When we finish with these guys, dying is gonna be the least of their worries."

"Let's take everything from them. We'll start by getting warrants to seize all of their belongings, and if any of the stuff they own is in their grandmother or mother's names we'll lock them up for life for laundering illegal funds."

"We'll lock up their kids' mother as well so no one will be around to take care of their kids, which means we'll end of locking them up too."

22

DELVIN MAYS, A SELF MADE MILLIONAIRE from selling drugs had never even caught a speeding ticket, so when two unmarked cars jumped behind him with flashing red and blue lights, he began to wonder if he had a busted tail light.

He calmly pulled over to the side of the highway, put his car in park and cut off the engine.

He sat calmly waiting on the agents to approach his care while tapping his fingers on the steering wheel.

Four agents got out of their vehicles and walked over to his car. And before he could roll his window down to ask them why he had been pulled over; they snatched him out of his car, laying him face down in the street with their knees in his back.

"What the hell is going on?"

He asked trying his best to stay calm. Agent Snail looked down at him and said,

"You're under arrest for the possession of a handgun used in a homicide last night and for over 5,000 grams of cocaine."

"What! You must be out of your damned mine, ain't no weapons in my car."

"You sure about that?"

The tall and slender Agent Fray said carrying a suitcase he planted inside of May's trunk came over to where he lay on the ground. Fray opened up the briefcase showing Delvin the five kilos of crack cocaine and the pistol whose serial number was scratched off, and all he could do was shake his head.

"Grab this piece of shit," Snail said, lifting him to his feet.

They carried Mays to the back of the cruisers and put him inside, closing the door. Then they all got back into their vehicles and drove off, leaving his car sitting on the side of the road.

Instead of going to Cook County Jail where they should have taken him, the Agents drove across the state line into Indiana, stopping at one of the federal hold-overs they often used to transfer prisoners from court or from one prison to the next.

"Where the hell are ya'll taking me?" Delvin asked as the car pulled into a garage that went straight up under the jail.

The two agents who were in the front of the car ignored him, as they made their way up to a booth where three armed federal officers stood. The officers checked the Identification of the two Agents while one of then ran a rod with a mirror at the end of it up under the car. After screening their identification and car to make sure that it wasn't rigged with explosives or any other dangerous weapons, the agents were allowed to drive through the check point.

They pulled into a parking space and got out of the vehicle.

One of the agents made his way around to the back door and opened it.

Delvin whose heart was pounding away at his chest and whose palms were sweating slowly, hesitantly made his way up out of the car.

"Come on!" Agent Swell who was two hundred pounds over weight said grabbing hold of his arm.

The other agent whose name was Yosh waited for the door to be opened then once it was he held it allowing Delvin and Swell to walk through. They entered a room in which they again had to wait to be buzzed into.

After going through another security check Swell and Yosh were forced to turn over their nine millimeter pistols, they all got on an elevator, taking it up to the fifth floor.

The two agents walked Delvin down the long, cold, quiet hallway until they reached a wall where over ten cells with old rusty bars were.

"We have one for holding." Agent Swell said to the man who stood behind the only desk in the room which was at the end of the hall.

The man who was a Deputy Sheriff made his way from around his desk over to where Delvin, Yosh and Swell stood. He quickly opened the cell door allowing for Delvin, who was so frustrated that he just wanted to rest, made his way inside the cell whose walls were covered in dried blood, roaches and feces that had been smeared everywhere.

He traveled over toward the steel-framed bunk bed, its mattress as thin as the toilet tissue it appeared someone had already used to wipe their butt with.

"Hey, come back over to the bars so we can get those cuffs off of you," Swell said, yelling over to Delvin, who just wanted to close his eyes so he could wake up out of this nightmare.

He traveled back over to the bars and stood looking at Yosh who said,

"Well turn around so we can get the damned cuffs off of your wrist."

"I don't know the procedure for this jail shit," Delvin, frustrated, said raising his voice.

He then turned around allowing the deputy sheriff to uncuff his wrist.

Before the three officers could move away from the cell, Delvin made his way over to the bed and climbed onto the top bunk which had a mattress that appeared to be cleaner than the one on the bottom.

He closed his eyes hoping he would be free again when he opened them.

"He's here," Fray said, peeping his head inside the door.

23

AGENT BELLY, THE LEADING FIELD AGENT for the FBI, and Shay, in charge of the team for Homeland Security, sat across from each other.

Without saying a word Belly waved Agent Fray off with his hand.

Once the door was closed Belly rose to his feet and unbuttoned his $1,500 hundred-dollar Armani suit jacket.

"We have to play this thing really smart or this kid is gonna walk and he's probably gonna sue the hell out of us for this as well."

"Relax," Shay said, opening up the folder on the table in from of him.

"He has no access to a phone, and since he's not in the county jail in Chicago, its highly unlikely that he knows anybody who will be able to get word to anyone he knows.

This is when we must be at our finest." He said tapping fingers on the table as he watched Belly paced back and forth.

"You need to relax, you're making me nervous."

"Think like a criminal, think like a criminal," Belly said, wiping his sweaty palms on the side of his pants.

Shay looked over at the door and motioned for Fray to open it.

"Bring him in, "he said, shuffling through the documents on his desk.

Agent Belly took a seat grabbing his briefcase and placing it on the table in front of him.

He opened it and removed a small recorder, placing it down on the table beside the briefcase. He grabbed a stack of pictures, placing them next to each other in front of him, closer to the middle of the table.

Just then the door opened and Fray came into the room escorting Delvin Mays.

"Have a seat." He said, forcing Delvin down into the chair in between Belly and Shay.

"Don't let me see you do that shit again," Agent Belly said, raising his voice as he got up from his seat pointing his finger into Fray's face.

"Now, get out!"

Fray quickly exited the room and disappeared from sight.

"Are you ok?" Agent Belly asked in a concerned voice, looking over at Delvin as he re-took his seat.

"Hell naw, I ain't ok! These crooked ass cops planted evidence in my vehicle after pulling me over illegally and they have yet to even give me one phone call!"

Shay who remained quiet pretended to write down all of Delvin's complaints as if documenting them.

"I'm sorry about all of that." Belly said trying his best to sound concerned.

"Mr. Mays, do you know any of these men?" Shay said, sliding the pictures across the table for him to get a closer look at them.

When Delvin saw the pictures of his brothers and four uncles his heart dropped but instead of telling the truth he lied.

"Naw! I don't know any of them." He said shaking his head.

"I have never seen any of them at all."

"I'm sorry you said that, Mr. Mays," Belly said, removing a stack of pictures from his briefcase.

He began showing Delvin the pictures of himself at the club and in several other places with all of the men.

"For someone not to know these guys, you sure are in a lot of photographs with them," he said, reaching for his recorder.

"Look, I know you wanna stay true to your family and be a real Honorable Gangster but you are about to go to jail for the rest of your life, and so far you don't even have to worry about the gun and drugs that Agent Fray and his team planted in your car, because you just lied to a federal agent which is a charge in itself," Shay said, looking into Delvin's face.

"Man, I told you I don't know them and I want my lawyer so this conversation is now over," Delvin said with a frown.

"Mr. Mays, before you get angry, I want you to know that we are only here to help you."

"Yeah, by locking my black ass up, that's how you're gonna help me, right?"

"We are simply trying to keep you from spending the rest of your life behind bars when it's not even you we want."

"All you have to do is name names. We don't even give a damn if you make up some shit, hell, most of the guys down at the Bureau call the stuff you guys testify to all bullshit."

"We have a name for it, which is called testi lying," Shay said with a smirk on his face.

"You think I'm stupid?" Delvin asked raising his voice.

"You don't have shit on me and you know it," he said, turning his head away from the two agents.

"I'll have my day in court and guess what, neither of you will determine the outcome of this. You're just a bunch of liars who try to divide and conquer."

Belly looked over at Shay who was beginning to think that they weren't gonna be able to flip Delvin.

"You think these people are gonna go to jail for you?" Belly said, pushing "play" on the small tape recorder he had cuffed in the palm of his hand.

As it played, Delvin listened to his uncle, cousins and brothers as they talked about buying drugs from him, hits they made for him and how close he was to all of the gang leaders in Chicago who bought thousands of kilos from him.

After watching Delvin's facial expression change for the worse, Belly pushed the "stop" button on the recorder and looked over at Delvin who he could tell was highly disturbed.

"You see Mr. Mays; everybody hasn't been keeping it as real as you think. They're all gonna walk on this Continuing Criminal Enterprise charge and you're the one who's gonna take the fall. You and your mother and grandmother and all three of your kids' mothers who have in one way or another aided your crimes by keeping quiet or by laundering your money."

"My family has nothing to do with anything, you idiots seem to think that I'm involved with, you hear me!" He yelled.

"Well we beg to differ." Belly said, removing several documents from his briefcase.

He then placed all of the documents in front of Delvin.

"This here is a receipt for a BMW. Here's one for a house, a Jaguar, another house." As Belly continued to flip through the documents, all with his mother's name Rose Cofield on them, his head began to spin.

"Here are a few homes and bank accounts that are in your grandmother's name as well."

"This is no proof of a crime," he said, sounding defeated.

"O yes it's very much proof of a crime," Mr. Mays, Shay said standing up.

"You see Mr. Mays, we have run your mother's and grandmother's entire financial history and we know for a fact that there is no way in hell either of these women or your kids' mothers can prove that they have worked for this money. That means that they have gotten this money illegally."

"Yes Mr. Mays, even if the attorney for the government can't prove that, they all will still be going to jail on tax evasion, which carries at least ten years. Do you think your eighty-seven-year old grandmother will survive after doing ten years in a federal prison?"

"Mr. Mays, doing life in prison or betraying a bunch of your family members who have already betrayed you is the least of your worries."

"Can you live with the fact that all your kids are gonna get raised by Pedophiles because their mommy and daddy, grandmother and great-grandmother are in jail?"

"They'll be forced to live in foster care or even worse, be adopted by sexual predators that I'm sure will have fun with those two beautiful little girls you got, Mr. Mays."

Delvin sat feeling dazed, and the more the agents talked the more he wanted to kill himself.

Both Shay and Belly got to their feet and Fray opened the door, stepping back inside the room.

"We are done with this clown," Belly said, looking over at Delvin as Fray grabbed his arm and lifted him to his feet from the chair.

"Now we are gonna go upstairs and give your uncles and brothers the same deal we just offered you and from the tape recording that you just heard, you know exactly what they're gonna do!"

Delvin made his way across the room to the door and once he was halfway through the threshold he stopped turning to Belly.

"Give me some time to think about it, "He said, as his eyes watered up with tears.

"Don't think about it too long or you'll have the rest of your natural life in a federal prison to think about it."

"You got two hours." Belly said watching as Fray removed Delvin from the room.

Once the door shut both Shay and Belly burst into laughter.

"That was a close one," Belly said, smiling.

"Tell me about it!" Shay said.

"That stuff about the Pedophiles raising his daughters is what really did it," Belly said.

"In less than an hour he'll be begging us to let us fuck him really good and hard."

After the cell door closed, Delvin walked over to the back wall of the cell. He was so gone mentally that he didn't even see the old black man sitting on the lower bunk. He began pacing back and forth in the cell and didn't stop until the old man shuffled over in front of him to use the rusty, smelly steel toilet attached to a sink that looked green inside.

The old man who had startled him pulled his pants down and took a seat on the toilet as Delvin just stood in the middle of the floor looking at him as if he was some sort of a figment of his imagination.

"Do you mind, I'm tryina take a shit here," the old man said, letting it rip.

Delvin who nearly threw up upon smelling the defecation, quickly covered his nose and turned around, heading back to the far wall.

"You've never been in jail before, have you?" the old man said, squeezing out more air and defecation. Delvin, completely numb, ignored him.

"Yeah, you never been in jail because if you have you'd know better than to turn your ass to a man who has his dick in his hands. Not only is it a good way to get raped, it's a good way for a fag boy to look at your ass while he jacks off to the thought of fucking you."

What the old man said triggered something in Delvin that Agent Belly said about his daughters.

In a rage he ran over to where the old man was sitting and began to beat him. The old man tried to cover himself but it did him no good. He began to scream for help but by the time the guards came he was unconscious, bleeding from his head, nose and mouth.

Two deputy sheriffs had to wrestle Delvin off of the man, but even after they had he continued to kick the man's unconscious body.

They cuffed him and took him out of the cell down the hall to another cell.

Enraged, he paced back and forth in the cell.

"Hey boy, all that anger ain't gonna make this situation go away," a man in the cell directly across from him said as he peered through the cell bars over to Delvin who appeared to be losing his mind.

"What the hell did you say to me?" Delvin said, stopping in his tracks.

"O yeah, that's it, Break the bars down and come over here and kill me!"

"Aww! Aww! Aww!" Delvin said, yelling at the top of his voice as he grabbed hold of the cell bars, shaking them.

"And the best drama and psycho Grammy goes to this idiot, "the man said.

"What the hell do you know?" You don't know shit, Delvin said, yelling over to the man.

"I know that you're in a bad situation that no amount of physical rage or money is about to get you out of. You see boy, the feds are the masters at finding what a man fears most and making him bend to their will in order for them to stop the pain they inflict upon everyone in our lives. It's the entire United States against you now, so you better understand that if you plan on keeping anything in life you ever loved."

As Delvin listened to the man an image of his grandmother dying in a jail cell came to his mind which made him fall to his knees, break down and cry. Right then he knew exactly what it was that he had to do.

24

WITH HIGH AMBITIONS OF ELIMINATING THE SIX AND FIVE POINT STAR FOREVER, which Little Devil, so close to achieving his goal of being King of all Kings and the only living God Gangster, had forgotten all about his little sister Ayana. She had been missing for two days, and he hadn't even noticed her absence.

"Felipia! Felipia!" an elderly woman who appeared to be in her late seventies cried.

She called out to him while making her way across the floor of the living room of his father's well-guarded mansion. Little Devil made his way to the third floor balcony. He grabbed hold of the railing, looking down at his grandmother Patricia, his only other love one besides Ayana. Patricia raised him herself.

"Felipia! She missing. He baby is missing," she said, looking up at him as tears streamed down her cheeks.

155

Little Devil, who had always been evil, non-remorseful and cold-hearted, felt a chill run down his spine and consumed his entire body. He had failed to do the one thing he was responsible for keeping the promise he had made to his father about protecting his sister. He wanted to speak but the site of the old woman he loved lying wailing on the ground choked him up. In a loud voice he yelled out Ayana's name, startling nearly all of the armed men in and outside the house. No more could be left to chance, he thought. Everyone who opposed him must die, and now it wasn't just for power, it was to fill the empty hole in his heart from the disappearance of his baby sister. He could only hope for his grandmother's sake that he could get her back safely. But with all the men he had killed, that was something he himself doubted; that even he, a God-Gangster, would be able to do.

25

IN A KINGS PIZZA UNIFORM, Denardo climbed out of his truck carrying two huge bags which appearing to hold several pizzas from Kings Restaurant, one of Little Devils favorite food spots. The gangsters standing on the corner immediately searched him and upon finding no weapons on his person or in the bags, they allowed him to pass. He made his way past the stone-faced Spanish gangsters who looked at him as if they wanted to murder him, and if he hadn't been making a delivery for their Lord, they would have. No black was stupid enough to show his face inside the Village and the fact that Denardo had, with all the wars raging throughout the city, made everyone standing out in the corridor that saw him very angry. The man standing guard by the front entrance of the building put his hand on Denardo's chest, preventing him from going any further. Another man, to his left pulled out a long-nose. 44 magnum revolver, and pointed it at Denardo's chest.

"No! Wait! He is here to deliver food for the Chief who is having a meeting upstairs. In less than thirty minutes, we'll kill him once he gets on the corner," the man said in Spanish to the other man, not knowing that Denardo understood every word. "Go ahead," the man who had stopped him said.

Denardo made his way inside the building, continuing on down the hallway until he reached the elevator. He pressed the button and waited. After three of the longest minutes of his life, the elevator door opened, allowing him to step inside. He quickly placed the two bags on the floor of the elevator and climbed up to ceiling, where he removed its cover. He grabbed the bags, scrambling into the elevator shaft where he began removing the pizzas from each of the boxes. He took the crust from around the pizza and began placing it in the corner of the elevator structure.

He climbed back down into the elevator and took it to the next floor. He continued to climb in and out of the elevator on each floor, lacing the walls of the building with the fake pizza dough which was actually Syntax C-4. After he had succeeded placing C-4 on every floor, he got back into the elevator taking it back downstairs. In somewhat of a rush, he bolted off the elevator and back down the hallway. When he was near the front door he was stopped by two gunmen. He stood watching as more than sixteen Disciples made their way up the steps past him. Unlike he expected, most of the men wore suits and looked nothing like the gangsters he had seen standing on the corners outside.

These men could have passed for lawyers and politicians which they really were, unbeknownst to Denardo. Once all the men had made their way up the steps, the two men let him pass, and then they climbed the stairs behind them. Denardo's heart was pounding and he quickly exited the building. He didn't even stop to look at all the hateful stares he had received just as on his way in. As he walked he could feel someone following behind him. It was the two men in front of the building who had plotted to kill him. He sped up trying to create some space between himself and them, but with the huge crowd of gangsters standing all over the projects, he was impeded from moving as fast as he would have liked. Just as he reached the corner nearing his truck, he noticed another cavalcade of at least twelve cars making its way up the street towards the building he had just left. He watched the faces of the two men that had following him who looked as if they just had seen a ghost.

They quickly turned around, disappearing into the crowd of men stationed throughout the village. Denardo watched as the cars slowly passed him and once the car in the middle (a black Maybach truck) was beside him it stopped and the back window rolled down. A man wearing shades peered over at Denardo while the man that sat beside him occupied himself with the laptop in his hand. The man smiled and the window rolled back up as the car drove off behind the rest of the cavalcade.

"Shit! Shit!" Denardo said, reaching in his pocket for his phone.

He quickly called Perrish saying

"He's not inside of the building!"

"How do you know?" she asked.

"Because I just saw him and I'm sure it was him," he said, making his way back into his truck.

He closed the door and started the engine, pulling away from the curb. As he did the two men that had been following him re-appeared out of nowhere.

"'Shit! Now somebody is trailing me," he said, stepping on the gas.

"Don't worry, I got them," Perrish said, firing on the two men from the roof across the street with a Remington 700.

When the bodies of the two men dropped those standing around began to panic.

With no concern for themselves they all ran over to the cavalcade and shielded it with their bodies. Denardo pulled to the corner and Perrish came running out of the building. She jumped into the truck and they sped off.

"Should I wait to blow the building?"

"No! Do it now and just pray that he's inside," she said,

He reached into his pocket and handed her the device that triggered the C-4. She looked over toward the middle building and pushed the button, watching as smoke rose from the middle of the neighborhood where the building had once stood.

They both continued to watch as the ground beneath them shook. The huge cloud of black smoke traveled through the buildings, nearly blinding them from seeing any further, nearly causing Denardo to crash the truck.

"Do you see that? No one in that neighborhood could have possibly survived," he said, grabbing hold of her hand.

"Let's just hope not," she said, looking into his eyes.

26

TWO DEPUTY SHERIFFS MADE THEIR WAY DOWN THE HALLWAY of the county jail escorting Delvin Mays back to the interrogation room where Shay and Belly were waiting.

When they reached the room they escorted him inside, and then left.

"So we assume that you are ready to talk," Belly said, watching Delvin as he took the seat between himself and Agent Shay.

"Yeah, Yeah, I got some stuff for ya'll, some real good stuff that I'm sure the President would give you both a mental of both honor for," he said looking nervous.

"So let's get started," Belly said, pushing "play" on the recorder.

"Look, the guys that you have been investigating are nobodies. I run all the drugs from Mexico into Chicago and all of the weapons that the gangs buy, so I know who's doing what and exactly how they're doing it. I can give you the ins and outs to the entire skeletal structure of Chicago gang life."

Belly looked over at Shay who crossed his legs as if to hide the hard he was feeling.

"Go on" Shay said, putting his right hand on his chin.

"Ya'll snatch me because ya'll know I know everything, right?" he said, playing reverse psychology with them.

They took the bait, both shaking their heads in agreement.

"Now give us some names," Agent Belly said, cracking his knuckles

"Man, I'm trying to tell ya'll that the real players don't go by names, they go by titles and ranks. The streets know them as Kings, Chiefs and Princes."

"Just give us the damned names!" Shay said, sounding frustrated.

"It doesn't work like that and ya'll know it. In order for us to do this, ya'll have to cut me free. None of my people know that ya'll have me, so I can still make the hundred million dollar gun and drug buys I got set up for tomorrow."

Both of the agents looked over at each other strangely.

"Look, there's a routine that we follow in order to keep things from going wrong and to keep the key players from ever getting caught, and that's what has been keeping you idiots from stopping us. The cartel we are dealing with to buy our guns and drugs are very careful. We only do business once a month on the 3rd day of the month, which is tomorrow."

"So even when you have the money and are out of guns and drugs needing more, they won't sell them to you?" Agent Belly asked, looking at him suspiciously.

"Exactly!"

"Tomorrow around 2 pm I pick up a pay phone down town in Chicago and say "Go."

"And what the hell happens after you say I Go?" Shay said, raising his voice.

"A package is taken to a building off 51ˢᵗ Street and dropped off. I never see who it is that drops it off because that's how they want it and that's how it has always been."

"Ok, so what's the name of the guy who is dropping off all this stuff?"

"Don't know," Devlin said, shrugging his shoulders.

"Man, this is a bunch of bullshit!" Shay said, slamming his fist down on the table causing the cup of coffee in front of him to spill.

"Now come on Mr. Mays, do you really expect me and Agent Shay to believe this fairy tale you are telling us?"

"Look, I don't give a damned what you and this idiot over here believes, it's true and the fact that you don't believe me tells me now why you losers that work for the government will never be on the same page as the gangsters that run this country's streets and neighborhoods."

"Ok, ok! Let's say you're telling the truth, how do you deliver the money to them?"

"The only time I see any of the men is when I go to deliver the money to them," he said, staring into Agent Shay's face

"The only problem is that every time the money is dropped off, a different Mexican picks it up. Now here's the other problem. How the hell am I gonna come up with the money by tomorrow when ya'll put me two days behind on my schedule?"

"Don't worry about the money, if what you are saying is true, we can get the Attorney General's office to give us the buy money." Shay said, still rubbing his chin.

"Look I'm gonna take a chance on you about this." Agent Belly said, looking into Delvin Mays' eyes to see if he could trace any sign that he might be lying.

"I'll have two agents follow you to the spot with the money and they're not gonna let you or the Mexican out of sight, you got that?"

"Yeah, I got that but ya'll can't be following me home, and if ya'll don't release me soon the plan won't work, because my babies' mothers are gonna start calling around to people I associate with looking for me. Hopefully nobody has seen my car sitting on the side of the road."

"Don't worry; we got your car downstairs in the parking deck. We are gonna let you go and you are gonna get up with us in the morning," Agent Belly said, standing up.

He walked over to where Delvin was seated and pulled a handcuff key out of his pocket, removing the cuffs from around his wrist.

"Don't try anything slick," he said, looking into Delvin's eyes.

"Now look, once you make contact with these guys we will come and wire you up and give you a half million dollars in marked US currency to make the controlled buy."

"No fucking way! That's not gonna happen!" Devlin said, jumping out of his chair.

"These ain't no dumbass stupid street punks that I deal with. These mutha fuckers are real Cartel boys!"

Upon hearing this, the two greedy agents turned to look at each other.

"So why wouldn't you be able to wear a wire?"

"Look man, these freaking Mexicans makes me walk through something like a metal detector that scans my whole freaking body for weapons and other things that I'm not supposed to have."

Agent Belly placed his hand on his right temple and began to massage. He then removes his glasses and stared over at Delvin, who looked as if he was scared to death.

"This is what we'll do. We're gonna release you and when these guys contact you or you contact them to make your next buy, you'll contact us and we'll give you the money to make the buy. You won't have to worry about being caught wearing a wire, we have ways around stuff like that. Here, sign this paper which states that now you work for us as a confidential source," he said, sliding a piece of paper that he had removed from his briefcase across the table over to Delvin.

He quickly signed the paper in front of him without even reading the first word.

"Damn, you're a real piece of work. You could have just signed your ass away," Agent Shay said with a smirk on his face.

He removed the paper from the table, placing it back into the briefcase.

Delvin, who had no intentions of doing anything with or for the feds, didn't give a damn what the he had just signed or said, because as far as he was concerned, just as soon as they let him go he was gonna disappear forever.

"Any shystie stuff and your grandmother will be the one paying the price," Belly said as Delvin slide past him through the door, exiting the room.

27

A THICK INTIMIDATING CROWD OF 4 CORNER HUSTLERS stood on the block covering every inch of the curb from Cicero to Madison Avenue on the Southside of Chicago. They all were standing with their weapons concealed, waiting and ready for a war to jump off.

Even from a distance the circle on Independence Avenue looked like fortress that could not in the least bit be penetrated.

If you weren't a Hustler you weren't going in or out of Hustler's turf.

The tension in the air throughout all the blocks that the Hustlers laid claim to was so thick that you had to breathe very slowly just to remain breathing at all. No one in the city was taking any more chances, and the gangs and their chiefs were all on high alert.

Little Devil (who had crowned himself The Devil) had accomplished part of his plan, which was to turn every one of the gangs against each other. He would then broker a deal with the smaller gangs until he consumed them and made them pledge a new allegiance to his new seven-point star and seven-point crown.

Those under the six-point star or the five-point star didn't trust anyone claiming anything different than their own set. This made the stars have little relevance, allowing The Devil to cause everyone to accept his seven-point star concept by choice or force.

28

DELVIN KNEW HE HAD TO SHAKE THE FEDS who were now following the cab they put him in.

When the cab reached the front of the crowded Daily Center, he hopped out of it and ran through the crowd as the two agents following him jumped out of their cars and attempted to pursue him. As he ran he stripped out of the orange jumpsuit he wore, becoming completely naked. He hopped a near-by fence and made his way down a long alley until he reached a door on the side of the building which he ran through. The two agents arrived at the alleyway but did not see him, which caused them to change direction. He made his way back out of the building on the other side, wearing a pair of baggy jeans and a shirt he had grabbed from the downstairs laundry room.

He flagged a cab down and jumped inside.

"Take me to Miller," he said, wiping the sweat from his face as he looked around to see if he was being watched. After driving for no more than fifteen minutes, the cab came to a stop in Gary, Indiana, right outside of a huge cornfield.

"Thanks," he said, stepping out of the cab.

"Hey buddy, pay me or I'll call the police."

"Look pal, if you wait for fifteen minutes I'll give you $5000.00 to take me back to the city."

The driver looked at him with skepticism on his face.

"What the hell do you have to lose? By the way, I'm not going far as you can see," he said, showing the man his bare feet.

"Ok buddy, I'll wait for you but if you're not back in fifteen minutes, I'm calling the police."

"Be my guest," he said as he closed the door and disappeared into the huge cornfield.

The cabdriver just shook his head, knowing there would be no way in hell the police would go into the cornfield looking for him, and neither would he, knowing that he would get lost forever.

After walking through the thick corn stalks, Delvin came upon a small river. Across the river there sat a tiny privately owned graveyard with no more than a hundred tombstones decorating its ground.

He traveled around to the far left of the river where it was most shallow, then waded into the water until he reached the other side.

He then traveled up into the graveyard, only stopping when he came upon a lot of tombstones at the very bottom of it.

The tombstones were surrounded by mud, barely remaining upright.

He looked around and quickly found a shovel which he used to dig up one of the caskets.

Anyone looking on would have thought he was a grave robber or a madman, but Delvin, busy digging in knee-high mud, didn't give a damn.

He dug and dug until he uncovered the casket. After dropping the shovel to the ground he fell to his knees and pulled it out of the hole. He opened it, removing two black duffle bags which he unzipped, checking their contents. Upon seeing all his money, he smiled. He reached into the bag and removed a set of car keys and a set of clothes, and began to quickly get dressed.

Once dressed, he tossed both bags over his shoulder and began to walk, making his way back toward the cornfield in the direction from which he had come.

He continued on through the field well-concealed by the cornstalks until he reaches a hidden blue C155 Mercedes-Benz, whose cover he quickly removed.

The car was spotless. He opened the door and jumped inside, using the key to start the engine.

Driving through the cornfield, smiling, knowing it wouldn't be long before he was in Canada where he would then take a plane to Afghanistan.

29

AFTER LOSING DELVIN, which was his only true lead to making the Rico Act, he was intending to indict the Chiefs of the cities' most ruthless gang, and both he and Agent Belly were scorned by their superiors.

In an attempt to rectify the mistake he had made by letting Delvin out of his sight, Shay decided that it was time to stop playing with the gangsters and apply pressure to their way of living.

Without saying a word to anyone he walked into the conference room, full of federal agents who had been waiting over thirty minutes for him to arrive.

He made his way to the podium at the front of the room, and then put down his briefcase while loosening his tie. After clearing his throat he glances over the crowd as they waited in anticipation for what he had to say.

"Ladies and gentlemen, we have a problem. We have groups of lawless individuals threatening the freedom of law-abiding citizens every day in one of the biggest cities in our nation. This city also happens to be the home of our sitting president, who has ordered the Attorney General of the United States to give us all the help we need to eliminate these gangs and their way of life."

Every face in the room stared back at him with a blank expression, uncertain of what was next to come.

"What I am telling you people is this: 'The Gloves Are Coming Off!' The City of Chicago is now a City under Siege! If anyone is caught in any neighborhoods of the inner city and are not on the Lease of one of the residents there, they are trespassing, which is probable cause to lock them up. You'll notice the folder that Agent Spike is passing out now contains the pictures, names and assets of nearly all the suspects I've obtained arrest warrants for. These men and women are to be considered armed and dangerous, and they are to be taken into custody A.S.A.P. You'll also find in this folder a list of assets, including cars, jewelry, houses, etc. that will be seized as well."

He addressed the crowd using an infrared pointer on the back wall where photos of the suspects were projected.

"We are dealing with ruthless organized gangsters who have been killing each other without hesitation, so it is safe to say that they will kill us as well, being that they hate us more than their fellow or rival gangsters. Everyone knows what is expected of them. Now fall out in teams and let's go kick some ass!"

In little or no time federal agents were running rampant through every project and street corner of the city of Chicago, arresting people and seizing their assets.

Another group of agents visited in local banks, forcing the managers to freeze the assets of these people as well. As sixteen teams of federal agents swept through the city making arrests, another twenty units consisting of more than 200 agents, set up cameras on every street light pole, set massive spotlights up and down every block. These were equipped with shot finders, which could tell the difference between a back-firing car muffler and any caliber gun and the distance and direction from which it was fired. Everyone in the city was under an eight o'clock curfew and anyone who violated the curfew didn't just end up in jail, they wound up in the hospital. People who had never owned an identification card were rushing to the Department of Motor Vehicles to get their ID because those who were caught on the street without it had to sit in the police precinct for hours.

Any resident caught selling drugs or possessing an illegal substance risked losing their Section 8voucher and being kicked out of the projects altogether.

It was starting to become virtually impossible for any of the gangsters to bang or fire their guns. The city had begun to look like a ghost town, except for the huge police presence on every corner; no one was hanging around outside anymore.

Those who were foolish enough to hang out on the blocks were surprised by a task force of police who bombarded their neighborhoods from every direction.

It was something that Agent Rumsfeld called

"All Hands On Deck."

30

"**YO MACK, THESE NIGGAS GONNA CAUSE US TO STARVE TO DEATH**" Blake said, looking over at his GD homie Mack G.

"No bullshit, somebody gonna have to show these pigs that we ain't about to go for this shit," he said, staring out from the window inside the gas station.

"Look Mack, we wouldn't even let gangsters and killers hold their nuts on us like this and we damned sure can't let these crooked -ass fagots with badges do the shit."

"You right!"

"Come on, we gonna show these bitches what we really do for a living."

Both he and Mack G got inside the car where they began loading their assault rifles they had stashed under their seats.

"Yo, be on the lookout for us to come through and once you see us, open fire on whatever vehicles you see following us." He said into his phone.

After starting his car's engine, he pulled out of the parking lot and headed down the street toward a group of federal agents who stood out on the street next to their unmarked vehicles.

As they drove past the agents both men stuck their weapons outside the window and opened fire without warning.

The seven agents didn't even have a chance. When the gunfire ceased, their bodies could be seen lying full of holes, bleeding on the ground next to their bullet-riddled vehicles.

As the vehicle sped off, more than six cars full of agents were in pursuit.

"Yeah nigga, did you see that shit!?" Mack G said, yelling and laughing at the top of his voice.

"These bitches followin' us lose them!"

"Naw, I ain't tryina lose them, we about to show these boys how we do shit around here in Chicago!"

Blake slowed down once he entered GD turf to let the agents think that they were gaining on them. He then drove straight up the hill into the projects and cut the car off.

He and Mack G jumped out of the car, breaking toward the building as the cars that were pursuing them came to a stop and the agents jumped out.

More unmarked cars also sped up the hill, not knowing that they were being lead into a death trap. Soon as Mack G and Blake were in front of the buildings out of reach of the gunfire about to erupt, the snipers that stood on the roof with their assault rifles rose up and began to open fire. The agents were trapped in a crossfire they hadn't seen coming.

A few of them took cover as they watched their fellow officers get chopped down by the rapid gunfire from the roof of nearly every building above them.

More officers showed up, and as they did their cars were fired upon while the agents inside were pinned down and slaughtered inside.

For hours the gun battle between the gangsters and the police went on and neither side was about to give up. Had it not been for the government calling in a helicopter to take out the snipers on the roof, more than half the agents would have lost their lives.

31

**GREEN ROCKS, WHO WAS THE CHIEF OF THE
VICE LORDS,** began reaching out to the other chiefs and
their Ahks and princes in order to come up with a way to
establish a cease-fire.

He knew that if they didn't call a truce or find a way to get
the feds off their backs, the lifestyle they had established
and came to love would soon no longer exist.

All of the chiefs were feeling the burden in blood and
treasure. The city under siege had completely stopped the
money they were used to seeing from flowing into their
coffers.

It was even worse after the assault that left the federal
agents dead a few days ago.

Many of the soldiers, who felt as if it were their chief's fault
that they were unable to pay their bills, began to go

renegade. It was well known to the soldiers on the street that the chiefs were too well off to starve and that made many of the soldiers declare their disloyalty.

32

THE SOLDIERS, who were now barely able to feed themselves or their families, began to realize how bad a position they were in.

It had become apparent to them that they had no power, not even enough power to pay their own bills.

On several occasions they voiced their opinions to their Ahks and princes which only seemed to fall upon death ears.

The Chiefs were able to broker a minor cease-fire between the major gangs but it seemed to have no benefit for the soldiers who were tired of sitting around waiting on orders of when and how they could move.

Many of the soldiers had brothers locked in prison that they were also taking care of, and without being able to eat the right way, the gangs in the jail began robbing each other which caused a huge riot to break out in Cook County Jail. More than twelve inmates were killed from being burned to death or stabbed. Without being able to pay for their lawyers, many of the gangsters were now forced to go to court with Public Defenders which resulted in many of them getting long sentences they could have avoided. Little Devil knew what effect all this trouble was causing and to make the other gangsters pledge loyalty to his seven-point star, he began paying for the lawyers of all the gangsters and taking care of their loved ones on the street.

In little or no time his twenty thousand man army grew to over 200,000 soldiers.

This made The Devil's Disciples the largest and most powerful gang in all Chicago.

Agent Rumsfeld had figured that the siege would cause many of the gangsters to start snitching but what it did instead was cause them to grow angry and pledge their allegiance to an even worse boss.

Throughout the jail more people were being jumped and stabbed to death. If you weren't claiming your allegiance to the seven-point star you weren't safe no matter who you were or what you claimed.

Agent Rumsfeld was still smiling but Mayor Growl wasn't. The City of Chicago was witnessing a recession. Without all the drug money flowing through the city, many businesses that had once been booming were now on the verge of bankruptcy.

Malls were empty and car dealerships were packed with new cars that hadn't left the lot since the beginning of the siege had started.

33

THE TASTE OF CHICAGO WAS NOT JUST ONE OF THE BIGGEST AND MOST LUCRATIVE EVENTS THROUGHOUT ALL OF CHICAGO; it was one of the most exciting and provocative tourist attractions in all of the United States.

Chefs from all around the world came to the Taste of Chicago once a year to display their most prized cuisine.

It was the only place you could find an Israeli Baker and a Palestinian Chef De Rang standing side by side, smiling all week long without attempting to kill each other.

The Taste of Chicago attracted the who's who of food lovers, including celebrities from every walk of life. On the early Friday morning at the start of the event, the aroma of exquisite foreign and American dishes could be smelled throughout all of Chicago.

Excitement and cheer filled the air, making it feel as if the war that was still raging within the inner city did not even exist. From his fifteen-story office window the Mayor looked down at the huge tents that had been pitched to accommodate both guests and residents attending the festival.

"This city will once again flourish into the great city that it was and always will be." He said, turning around to face his deputy Marion Maynard.

"Yes sir it will. Gangsters like Al Capone couldn't even stop this great city of ours from being what it is today and neither will a bunch of street punks with automatic weapons."

"You're damned right they won't, that's why I have ordered Chief Harpo to surround this event with over 5,000 of our finest police."

"If a rat even runs in and out of a sewer I wanna have it known. We can't afford to allow this event to be affected by what's going on within the inner city." He said, looking over at his chief deputy with rage in his eyes.

"If one of these punks wipes his ass I wanna know about it, you got that?"

"Yes sir, I got that."

"This is our city, not theirs, and by God I'll be damned if I let these cowards keep me from being re-elected come November. I have dreams of one day being president of this great nation of ours, and if anything goes wrong throughout this week I have to kiss that dream of mine goodbye."

"Sir, trust me! Nothing is going to happen."

"You damned well better make sure of it and have the National Guard on standby just in case it does."

"Sir, we have nearly every street under tight security. No one can ever leave their apartment without us knowing about it."

Hearing that caused the mayor to smile.

"It's about time that good people of Chicago and this government have control of our city streets again."

"That damned Hoover fella had become a god. Damned Michael Jordan and the rest of them. Every damned kid in American now wants to be the next King Larry Hoover."

"It's not gonna happen, not on my watch! You got that?"

The Mayor said pointing his finger in his deputy's face as his white face turned beet red.

As they both began to walk out of the office the mayor shook his head while putting his arm around his deputy.

"I just can't believe this shit. On the streets this guy was a warlord and a gangster, in jail he's a King, and in death he'll probably be a Martyr bigger than Bin Laden."

34

A DARK-SKINNED, HEAVILY TATTED GANGSTER STOOD HOLDING AN UMBRELLA FOR THE DEVIL.

"Boss the other chiefs have asked me to see if you would be willing to meet with them."

Without even turning to look at him, The Devil, staring out at Lake Michigan while skipping fifty cent pieces began to sneer.

"Men don't meet The Devil until after their demise. It'll be a cold day in hell when this war ends."

While he was lowering the smoke dark Prada shades from over his bloodshot red eyes so that Terror, his hit man and closet body guard could see them.

"Fire consumes everything it touches, so it is only when the entire underworld has been scorched by my wrath and the chiefs have submitted to my agenda that I will stop unleashing hell upon them."

He then joined his hands together, interlocking his fingers and raising them high, showing the men watching him his seven-point star that represented the new nation which he was building.

"So many of our own have died as well though my lord," Treacher, another of his bodyguards who stood close to his right hand side said while looking down at his own feet.

"For every one of my Disciples that have given their lives, a thousand men have joined our cause and fifty have died in their place."

"Soldiers die and this is what they are created to do, as Kings are meant to rule, which you shall see me do. When men are not living up to the reason for which they were created, then they are in Hell already."

"I have news of Ayana, my lord," another of the men who had just gotten off his cell phone said, making his way through the crowd getting closer to The Devil.

Upon hearing Ayana's name The Devil's entire facial expression changed.

"We have news and proof that she is still alive but we still have no knowledge of her whereabouts."

The Devil remained silent, concealing his thoughts. Although he was very sad about Ayana being kidnapped, he was hoping for news of her death. This way his enemies would have no other way in the world to hurt him and once the only part of his heart that was still living had died he would have no mercy upon mankind ever again.

35

"BABY ARE YOU OK?"

Perrish, who lay in the bed behind Ayana asked. She uncovered her face which was covered by her long curly jet black hair.

Without answering a word, Ayana shook her head yes.

She then turned to face Perrish.

"Do you think my Dad is in heaven?"

"Well, Yes. Your daddy was a very loving good man, so I can't see why God wouldn't have allowed him into heaven." She said, smiling.

"If my father was The Devil, how could he be gone to heaven when the Devil's place is Hell?"

The question made Perrish look over toward the door where Denardo stood watching them. "Heaven and hell are what you make them." He said, making his way into the room.

When he reached the bed in the middle of the floor he stopped, leaning down to kiss Ayana upon her forehead.

"Is hell better than heaven?"

"I sure would like to believe so." He said, wrapping his arms around Perish who smiled up at him while pulling tiny Ayana to her chest.

"Is my brother gonna take me from you, Perrish?"

"No, he's not gonna take you from me. No one is ever gonna take you from me."

"I don't wanna go with Felipia, he scares me." She said, tucking her head into Perrish's chest.

Perrish looked over at Denardo.

"We'll never let anyone take you anywhere. You're our baby and we intend to keep you safe from everyone you don't want to be around."

Ayana looked over at him and smiled as she grabbed hold of his hand which was wrapped around Perrish's waist.

Denardo kissed the back of Perrish's neck, taking his arms from around her, standing up from the bed. He looked back at both Perrish and Ayana, then he made his way back out into the dark hallway going down the hall toward the steps where he had a mini-AK waiting.

36

IN A FILTHY, COLD, BARELY LIT WAREHOUSE, The Devil watched on in amusement as two of his Disciples tortured sixteen rival gang members.

He had put bounties on every gangster in the city's head who refused to accept or ride under his seven-point star.

The screams of the men echoed throughout the huge empty warehouse falling upon deaf ears.

There was no one to help them and neither could they be saved.

The two men used pliers to pull the men's' teeth from their mouths as their boss watched,

They even attached jumper cables to their testicles and fried them, causing some to pass out.

A man dressed in all black carrying a black briefcase made his way across the warehouse floor, escorted by three armed men who all made their way towards The Devil, who sat upon an old pool table watching as his men hung the men high on iron hooks.

The man in the suit whose name was Raynosa carefully stepped over a huge puddle of blood trying not to get his Ferragoma leather shoes soaked in the crime scene.

"What news do you have for me about my sister Raynosa?" The Devil asked, turning to face him and the other three men who were escorting him.

Raynosa, The Devil's lawyer, swallowed hard then placed his briefcase on the table next to The Devil. He then opened it removing a shiny disc. Without speaking he walked over toward a huge television that sat not far away from them near the middle of the floor.

Raynosa placed the disc into the DVD player, and then pushed "play," turning up the volume on the television.

A clear image of Ayana was present on the screen. She sat unhurt, dressed in the same clothes she wore on the day of her abduction.

The camera went off Ayana for a brief moment and it came back to her sitting naked, crying.

The Devil could feel the anger boiling up inside of him. He couldn't even imagine someone molesting his little sister.

Killing her was one thing but keeping her alive and causing her to suffer was another.

A muffled voice could be heard on the screen.

The voice of what was more than likely the kidnapper's began making demands. It swore if he didn't follow them his sister would be molested and tortured every hour of every day for the rest of her life.

The Devil, who had always figured himself to be heartless, nearly came to tears upon listening to his little sister cry while looking at her face.

He got up from where he was sitting on the pool table and went over to the television, placing his hands over the screen, running them over her beautiful, small innocent face, and then a single tear fell from his right eye.

He then turned back to Raynosa and said

"These people should know better than to ever try to make a deal with The Devil. My sister is now dead to me and shall be those who have kidnapped the only living piece of my heart."

The men who stood around in the warehouse had no idea how ruthless their boss truly was. He had turned his back on the only chance he would ever have to get his sister back and this even disturbed Raynosa who had been his father's family lawyer even before he himself had been born.

To Raynosa, a man's honor was everything and what The Devil was showing him was that that he had no honor at all.

Raynosa, who was highly disturbed by The Devil's reaction, excused himself, leaving the same way that he had come in.

Although he was a lawyer now and one of the best in the city that was politically connected, he still had a gangster deep down inside of himself.

Before he had passed the bar exam he and The Devil, Little Devil's father, were right-hand men.

He knew that his old friend would have never approved of the way his son was acting, especially when it came to the way he was treating family. As a lawyer Raynosa had seen both sides of the law, and was able to say that he lived both sides of the streets so he knew too well how quick men were to die for their dignity, honor, respect, money and power.

He saw how the poorest man on earth could feel like the richest as long as he was able to be respected and honored by his peers.

He also was disturbed by how the attitude of the men in the streets had changed.

There was no longer any honor at all amongst thieves.

History had begun to repeat itself right in front of his eyes.

Just as the cowboys of the Wild Wild West had done in their time; the men in the streets were again beginning to do.

It was nothing for an outlaw who had robbed stagecoaches and banks for a living or went about raping woman and ravishing every town he passed, to pick up a badge and become a sheriff and law enforcer once he was being pursued by the law for his crimes.

In the time of Wyatt Earp and Jack Holiday, picking up a badge and becoming a sheriff was the norm and now he was again seeing that it was becoming the norm for the criminals who got caught doing wrong as well.

As a lawyer he was able to see strong men at their most vulnerable point. He was able to see the men whom the streets honored and worshipped do things no one would ever figure they would do.

He noticed how the men with nothing but their honor were willing to sit in jail for life while those at the top who had houses and money were usually the first to tell.

Was it because those with nothing but their honor weren't so willing to give up all they had while those with everything weren't?

It's a saying that goes "the bigger you are the harder you fall," and those at the top usually had a lot further to fall making their fall much harder to bear.

Men who he knew were capable of doing twenty years still chose to tell, out of plain selfishness, while others told just to pay those back who shot at them, tried to kill them or owed them money. Many others didn't tell and it wasn't always because they were remaining true. Plenty of times it was simply because they themselves didn't have anything or anybody to tell on.

Prison was something that caused the strongest men to break and a man doing a ten-year sentence wasn't the same man when he was doing a fifty-year sentence.

When a man was faced with a choice of losing the only life he would ever live on this earth to prison, and \never again touching a woman or living free, versus losing his respect and honor many of those men chose not to be respected or honored at all.

If there had ever been such a thing as a rule to the lawless, treacherous street life, the outlaws and gangsters were now choosing and picking which of them they themselves chose to abide by.

To a drug dealer or common crook with wealth, it was nothing to relocate himself and his family and start over, but to a man who had nothing, and had to face the same people he had chosen to betray, he risked losing everything.

All in all, the greatest thing that Raynosa had learned from being a lawyer was that no gangster rich or poor wanted to accept the fact that eventually everybody had to pay the piper. To a man doing a life sentence, facing life in court wasn't the same as actually having to live in prison for rest of his life. It was just like when a wild animal in the jungle was taken out of its environment, men of the wild had trouble surviving outside of their elements and neither did they choose to do so.

Those who were forced to do so often faded away in mind, body and soul and began to do things even they doubted they were capable of doing.

He had seen men five times more treacherous than Little Devil fold like a paper napkin upon the weight of a life sentence in federal prison.

No lifer wanted to be doing a life sentence no matter how much they knew that they deserved it.

As a gangster he could not understand why prison made men break, but as a lawyer it was as clear to him as the moon above.

Men who had believed themselves capable of weathering the storm often got blown away by the winds when that storm came.

Some men killed with no remorse in the streets while others were incapable of even hurting a soul. Some men were able to have their way with any woman of their choice while others spent years hustling never to even get past the three point five grams of drugs they had started off with.

All men were not created equal although they believed themselves to be. A man barely even knew his true strengths until he was tested. If a man had no true knowledge of what he was capable of, how could he ever know for sure what the next man was capable of as well?

The gangsters of old and those of new all seemed to suffer the same disease. They all expected from others what they were incapable of giving or unwilling to give.

In the movie The Matrix, Morpheus said something to Neyo that Raynosa seemed to always think of when he thought of men like The Devil, and so many others who believed themselves to be tougher and meaner than they actually were; Morpheus told Neyo that "It was a difference between knowing the truth and living the truth."

The question was whose reality were most people even living by?

37

PLEAS TO BRING ABOUT A CEASE FIRE CONTINUTED TO FAIL, every time they were mentioned. The Devil, who now controlled nearly the entire city, wanted nothing to do with ceasing the war he had declared upon the other gangs and their Chiefs.

Loyalty was now just a word that meant nothing to anyone. The gangsters were starving and the only ones they declared their loyalty to was themselves or those who were helping to feed them and their loved ones.

Agent Rumsfeld had succeeded at stopping the buying and selling of drugs, but it did not in the least bit stop the crime which seemed to surge.

Robberies, home invasions, and murders were now at an all-time high in the city. Instead of starving the beast and causing it to tire and become weak, the government simply drove it mad and now it was dying to feed no matter how it had to.

In broad daylight at its busiest time, grocery stores and jewelry stores were being robbed by villains with little remorse. The gangsters and villains were now finding a way to exploit the high police presence which occupied the ghetto streets on a daily basis.

While the cops were busy patrolling their turf the gangsters were busy terrorizing the neighborhoods of the law-abiding citizens the police were now too preoccupied to protect.

As they both rode in a stolen two-door Chrysler 300, Mack G and Blake had only one thing on their minds and that was getting paid.

"These muthafuckers living real good on this side while we around the way starving."

Mack G said, blowing the huge cloud of weed smoke from his mouth and nose while passing Blake the huge marijuana-packed cigar he held in his hand.

"Yeah, yeah. I told you these white people was living really good out here in the hundreds."

Blake, who was driving, made a sharp left onto a residential street that looked as if it should have been well-guarded but there were no police in sight.

"I told you that all police were too busy harassing us to be up here guarding these good people's shit," Mack G said, laughing out loud as he humored himself.

Blake pulled the car to the side of the road and parked and both he and Mack G got out, they approached the unguarded huge fence.

They hopped the gate, dropping down over to the other side and into the very well-to-do neighborhood, and then quickly made their way past the first house and down the street.

"This some real nice shit." Mack G said admiring the lovely houses they passed on both sides.

"Yeah, here were go, right here" Blake said, heading up into the driveway of the fifth house on the left.

"You sure this that senator fella's house?" Mack G asked as Blake nodded his head without saying a word.

"And you're also sure that he and his family are gone?"

"They damned sure better hope so," Blake said, making his way over to the door which he quickly picked, causing it to unlock.

Once the door's lock was off he pushed the door open, making his way inside with Mack G following him. The inside of the house was quiet, and for a moment it seemed as if no one was home. The two men continued on through the house, admiring the lovely things they intended to take once they had gotten what they had originally came there for.

Blake stepped through the threshold of the den into the kitchen, and that's when he saw something that made him stop in his tracks. A man with grayish hair and three females were sitting at the table. The youngest of the three females, who appeared to be no older than sixteen, began to scream at the sight of Blake and Mack G, causing the others to turn their attention to where both Mack G and Blake stood.

Both men pulled out their weapons with the intention of only trying to intimidate the family but before they could grab anyone to silence them, the pretty sixteen-year-old girl jumped up from the table and ran.

"Wait! Wait," Blake screamed, trying to stop her as Mack G took off after her.

Before anyone else could do the same, Blake ran over to the table and smacked the senator across his head with the butt of his gun, causing blood to gush from his head as he fell to the floor.

The other two women began to scream.

"Shut the fuck up before I kill this mutha fucker," he said, pointing the gun into the elderly man's face.

The two women, who were still crying, tried to calm themselves in hopes of not provoking him into killing anyone. In the distance that young woman who had run from the table could be heard screaming, making the woman begin to cry.

"Shit!" Blake said, looking over toward the direction from which the constant screams were coming.

"Get on the ground, both of you, hurry up and get on the ground, face down!"

The two women did as they were ordered to do and once they were on the floor he used the rope that he cut from the window shades to tie their hands. Helpless, the two women continued to cry, fearing for their lives and the lives of their father and niece who stopped screaming.

After securing everyone in the kitchen, Blake walked through the house to find Mack G.

When he reached the basement he froze in horror at what he saw in front of him. A completely nude Mack G lay on the floor between the young woman's bare thighs, ravishing her viciously.

From the cut across the young girl's neck, from which a puddle of blood had already poured out onto the ground, Blake could tell that she was dead or going to die soon.

"Stupid mutha fucker, this ain't what we came here for," he said kicking Mack G in his ass.

"You stupid horny clown, you just fucked up everything!"

Mack G continued to pump away at the lifeless body of the beautiful young woman until he climaxed. He then pulled himself out of her and rose to his feet, wiping the sweat from his head.

He pulled his pants up and before either of the men could turn around they heard the screams of one of the women coming from the door behind them. Upon seeing her niece lying on the ground raped and dead, the woman collapsed.

"How the hell did she get loose?" Blake said out loud, speaking to himself.

He quickly ran back to the kitchen and what he saw caused his heart to drop.

The second woman was gone and so was the old man. The phone was sitting on the table off the hook, and in the distance he could hear sirens.

"Shit!" he yelled, turning to look back at Mack G who had begun stripping the woman who had fallen to the floor unconscious intending to rape her as well.

Blake pointed his weapon toward him and fired, striking him in the back of his head three times. His lifeless body fell on top of the woman he was inches from penetrating.

Blake ran toward the back of the house and opened the window. He then climbed from it, tossing the gun back inside near Mack G's dead body. He then turned around and took off running at full speed.

He hopped several fences, ducking behind garages and after making it a distance from the house he began to feel a sense of joy come over him. He had made it away from the crime scene.

He wiped the sweat from his face and removed his blood-stained hoodie, dropping it to the ground next to his feet. He then left from behind the garage in which he had taken cover, heading over toward the front fence. As he crossed the street he picked up his stride, feeling like a free man who gotten away with murder.

He traveled down the street and as he was about to turn the corner two police cruisers pulled onto the street.

He turned to run and that's when he saw a huge police presence coming towards him on foot. In an attempt to escape he reached for the Ruger 9 millimeter he had tucked into the small of his back, but before he could get off one shot, the officers opened fire in his direction, killing him instantly.

38

AS THE PEOPLE WENT ABOUT THEIR BUSINESS enjoying all of the many fantastic cuisines from all over the world, a huge squad of police stood near every side street eating free plates of food they had been given while drinking Heineken and other expensive and exotic beers out of their coffee mugs.

The people were having so much fun at the event that they barely even noticed the huge police presence all around them.

Celebrities as well as common folks sat eating as they listened to music being played by live bands.

Beautiful women strolled every inch of the ground as men tried their best to get their attention. Everybody who was anybody was present at the Taste of Chicago which was a rare event that couldn't be matched by any of its kind.

Chefs passed out testers of everything they cooked putting a smile on every face that passed by their venues.

Every food from every corner of the world could be found between the venues which amounted to more than 8,000 in number.

Children smiled, played and laughed as their parent's devoured exquisite cuisine just as if they were traveling through every corner of the known world.

39

DRESS IN ALL BLACK SOILED CLOTHING, Screw Blood walked up the deserted side of Michigan Avenue pushing a shopping cart which appeared to be full of cans and other garbage.

His scuffed-up, untied boots, which appeared to be four sizes too big for him, dragged on the ground while nearly flopping off his feet.

His dingy, long dreadlocks had grass, straw and dirt all over them, making it look as if he had just awaken after taking a nap under the bridge.

"You see this dirty piece of shit." one of the officers said as he watched that figure which appeared to be a hopeless bum making his way toward the wooden barrier they stood behind.

"Yeah, we see him. Every year the aroma from the

taste brings every animal out of the sewers," another one of the officers said, causing his brothers in arms to laugh.

"This guy looks like a super bum," another of the officers said after taking a swig of beer from his mug.

"Hey fella, the party stops here," another one of the officers said.

He was close to the wooden barrier that divided the street.

The figure who appeared to be staggering drunk ignored him as he continued to get closer to the barrier.

This caused the officer to pull his nightstick from his side.

He looked back at the others and smiled saying;

"Looks like we're gonna Rodney King this here fella, and with all the residents over at the festival there won't be a soul to catch it on camera."

"Hungry sir, feed me" Screw Blood said as he did his best to play his character which had all of the officers fooled.

"I said get your stinking, filthy black ass on, boy!" The officer said, smacking his night stick down on the wooden barrier which caused a loud thud.

This caused Screw Blood to raise his head up. He quickly looked over all the weapons each of the officers were carrying in their holsters and in their hands.

He noticed that most of the weapons were handguns like .38 revolvers, glock forties and 9 millimeters. A few of the officers held riot shotguns but only two of them had assault rifles. He knew that those officers would be the first that he would have to take out.

"I warned you, now you're gonna pay, boy!" The officer said as he began to place his leg over the barrier.

Screw Blood began to whistle and when he had finished his twin brother Maniac Seville raised up out of the shopping cart with a .20 millimeter Gatlin gun sending the cans flying all over the place. The officers stared on in horror, thinking that they were in some sort of bad dream. They didn't even have a chance. Maniac Seville opened fire with the powerful weapon which scraped the people closest to the barrier away like twigs caught in a windstorm.

He continued to fire as the rest of the officers ran for their lives screaming. Many of them took shelter behind their vehicles and a huge police trailer which was parked in the middle of the street. The Gatling gun swept every inch of the street, and when Maniac Seville had stopped firing nothing was left standing-not even the police cruisers or the trailer which the Gatling gun had completely sawed in half.

The two twins took off running. Once they reached State Street, they hopped inside their getaway car, a black Tesla, which was parked on the side of the road with the engine still on. They watched as huge crowds of panicking pedestrians came running from every direction in fear of their lives.

People were trampling over each other while parents were being separated from their children.

Screw Blood laughed, saying "Look Star!" as his twin stepped on gas flying down State Street.

For a moment they had felt like they had gotten away clean until they reached the highway where several police cruisers were waiting for them.

Screw Blood slid up in his seat, sticking his arms and torso out of his window as Maniac Seville passed him the Saw M-2-4-9 Assault Rifle which he had to hold onto the roof of the car to keep from falling over.

He took aim on the Barricade and fired. The Saw caused the trunks and engine of the police cars to explode, sending the police who stood near them fleeing for their lives.

The Tesla slid past them through a narrow gap. Screw continued to fire on the police cars.

They followed him as they sped down the highway. Maniac swerved in and out of traffic, putting the lives of innocent pedestrians at risk.

Screw, who could see that no matter how fast they went they wouldn't lose their tail, began to fire at the cars of pedestrians which caused a huge pileup of cars in the middle of the highway. Cars were swerving into concrete barriers on the side of the road and exploding.

This prevented the police from following them, but a helicopter that had appeared out of nowhere still was hovering above.

"Shit!" Screw said, firing up in the sky towards the helicopter which changed its direction to keep from being hit by the oncoming gunfire. Maniac made a sharp left off of the highway as Screw opened fire on a sixteen-wheeler, causing it to flip over several time before it exploded.

As the Tesla made its way through the city blowing through every red light, a few police cruisers continued to pursue it.

Maniac Seville made a left then sharp right coming upon a school where a crowd of children were about to cross the street. Screw opened fire which caused the kids to panic and they did exactly what he had expected, which was run in every direction.

Maniac had to swerve several times to keep from hitting the kids who were running through the street. As the officers reached the part of the street where the kids were, the slowed down all together which allowed for the two brothers to get away.

In order not to be spotted by the helicopter again, Maniac Seville pulled the Tesla into a garage under a nearby building.

They both got out of the vehicle, and then Screw Blood dosed it with gasoline then set it on fire as they both walked away unharmed.

40

UPON ENTERING HIS HOUSE RAYNOSA MADE HIS WAY INOT THE LIVING ROOM...where he removed his coat then picked up the mail from the table where it sat, As he flipped through the mail he noticed a red dot on his chest which caused him to look up. Out from behind the window curtain Denardo appeared in all black.

"Don't move to fast and don't speak to loud or those 7 disciples outside will come in here to find your brains splattered all over that Picasso on the wall behind you. Have a seat."

Raynosa did as he was told and set down. He then placed the mail back down on the table and raised his hands so Denardo could see he wasn't trying to reach for anything.

"So what do you intent to accomplish by this?"

"I'm asking all of the questions!" Denardo said making his way closer to him. He reached the brief case he had in his left hand over and Raynosa took it.

"Open it!"

Raynosa opened the case after placing it down on his lap. in the case was three million dollars and a note. He picked up the note and began reading it.

"So you really expect me to get all of the chiefs to agree to meet me?" He asked as he closed the brief case back and locked it.

"The money is for you to make sure they do just that. Two million for them and the other million is for your services. We realize lawyers in this city aren't cheap. Perrish wants the generals that surround The Devil to know they have three million reasons not to cross her."

Raynosa stood placing his over coat back on. He looked at Denardo and said "I can make this happen."

Perrish who sat hidden from view watched as her little brother M-Jettic checked the book shelf. He removed one of the books taking the note she had left for him out of it. after reading it a tear fell from his eye.

He and his sister hadn't been close since his father's death but he loved her the same. He knew that they couldn't be seen together but as soon as all of this madness was over he knew she would be safe.

As he crumbled the letter into a ball he looked around hoping to see her and when he didn't he turned to walk away. Perrish hoped that her brother headed her message. she hoped that he wouldn't be stupid enough to go to the meeting with the other chiefs when she had told him not to.

41

WHAT HAS SEEMED TO BE WORKING IN AGENT RUMSFELD'S WAR ON THE GANGS INSIDE OF CHICAGO had only seemed to cause more damage and lead to the death of more people then it had previously. The gangsters hadn't tucked their tails between their legs and run as he had expected then to do. Instead they turned their anger on the city itself, causing more pedestrian causalities then at any other time.

As he watched CNN from his office television screen, Agent Rumsfeld couldn't help but think that soon he would be the next to be sitting before Congress trying to explain how the siege had gotten out of hand.

He had failed to factor in one thing in all of his brilliant planning, and that was that the city of Chicago was America's Gangland and always would be.

As his phone began to ring jerking him out of the blur he had slumped into, an idea came to his mind.

"Kill the head the body shall fall." He said, nearly in a whisper.

"What did you say, sir?" Agent Nolesky who stood near his desk on his right-hand side asked.

Rumsfeld smiles a sadistic smile while looking up at him and said,

"Kill the heads and the bodies shall fall."

On the other side of town The Mayor of Chicago wasn't smiling at all. He stood on a stage behind a podium sweating bullets as news reporters grilled him on why so many pedestrians and officers had been slain in the last few days.

There were questions ranging from:

"How the hell did two men get away?"

"How was it possible that anyone in Chicago was safe when ruthless gangsters were allowed to run around with high-powered military style weaponry, reaping havoc on the city streets?"

The Mayor, who couldn't come up with one good answer, just did the best thing for him, to do at the time, which was let his head, hang.

42

SINCE HE OR ANY OF HIS AGENTS WERE UNABLE TO TRACK DOWN THE DEVIL to bring him in for questioning, Agent Rumsfeld thought of the next best thing. There was only one person in the city of Chicago with enough power to stop the war which was raging through the city and that person was already doing over six life sentences in the Fed's for all types of crimes.

The man who Agent Rumsfeld knew could stop the war just by picking up the phone in his ADX Supermax cell wouldn't speak to the President of the United States, so they had to settle for second best which was Fennyman, the Prince of all Princes.

Fennyman, who was also headed to the ADX in Florence, Colorado, had been in Diesel therapy ever since the start of the siege by Agent Rumsfeld's request.

Diesel therapy had been designed to cause the toughest of men to break, but Fennyman wasn't a man to be broken for any cause.

In less than a two-month period he had been transferred to over two hundred county jails on all sides of the country.

One day he would wake up and it would be sunny and the next day he woke up it would be raining or snowing.

Being transferred from place to place made it impossible for anyone to contact him. His mail never seemed to catch up to him and he never stayed in any of the jails long enough to order cosmetics or food, which had him looking and smelling like a bum.

He had been sent through the Transic Center in Oklahoma so many times that those who seen him and didn't know him swore he was snitching on everyone. The feds intentionally kept him away from everybody from Chicago knowing that he could send words to his people through them.

He was being feed unseasoned, nearly uncooked food, which caused him to lose over a hundred pounds, making him look much frailer than he really was.

When the Marshals saw that diesel therapy couldn't break him they placed him in county jails in New Mexico and West Virginia, which had a high presence of Arian brothers, dirty white boys and Piasas, but on finding out who he was, none of the men dared to touch him, fearing starting a war that they knew would be no good for anyone.

Agent Rumsfeld was constantly being briefed on his conditions finally decided to see him face to face, so he ordered him to be brought to the federal center in Chicago.

As he stood in his cell shirtless and doing super burpies, the Special Housing Unit Lieutenant banged on the heavy metal door, causing him to turn to face the door.

"You have a visitor, so get dressed," Lieutenant Maze said, stepping away from the door.

Fennyman stopped doing burpies and made his way over to the metal sink which was attached to the metal toilet. He thought about grabbing the knife he had made but relented.

He then grabbed the toothpaste and toothbrush off the sink and began brushing his teeth.

After washing his face he got dressed in the prison jump suit which hung across his bunk.

Before he had finished getting dressed, four officers and the lieutenant came back, opening up the food slot in the middle of the door.

"Turn around and put your hands through the slot," the lieutenant ordered, and he complied.

Once he was cuffed, a belly chain was slid around his waist. His door was opened and a leather belt with a shocking device was placed around him. One of the officers placed shackles around his feet and then he was escorted out of the block by all five men. Once they reached the hallway which was cleared of all people, an officer carrying a loaded shotgun began following behind the crowd.

After traveling for about five more minutes through tunnels that appeared to be under the ground, he was escorted into a private room where three agents sat waiting for him.

"Fuck naw! I ain't going in there, I ain't got shit to say to you fucking feds," Fennyman said, struggling to make his way back out the door.

The five officers tried to subdue him but he was too strong. He broke away and was making his way back down the hallway when the officer that held the shotgun struck him in the back of the head, knocking him to his knees.

"You bitch mutha fucker," he said, spitting the blood that filled his mouth onto the floor next to him.

The other five officers attacked him and began to rough him up. Once he was lying face down on the floor they dragged him back into the room where Agent Rumsfeld sat with the ATF Agent Smacks to his left.

They placed him in the seat across the table where he sat slumped with murder in his eyes.

"You're one tough mutha fucker, aren't you?" Agent Rumsfeld said, getting up from the table. He traveled over to where Fennyman sat slumped in his seat and placed his hand on his shoulder.

"I hear that you have an appealing that's looking really good. It would be a shame if that appeal kept getting taken off the court's docket sheet after waiting to be heard after all these years."

"Damn you, you can't do shit about my appeal, and like I told your sucka ass eight years ago, I'll be back on the streets soon and it didn't take me snitchin to get there, either."

"Yeah, you're a real tough gangster, which I can attest to. Too bad your homies aren't cut from the same cloth."

"Why the hell am I even here?"

"I told you that our appeal was coming up so I decided to carry you through Hell before you got released if in fact you get released. Right now I have this entire city under siege, so if you even blink the wrong way your trifling ass will be back in jail so fast that you'll think a shooting star shot up your ass. I just wanted to tell you face to face who's running this city now. It's not yours any longer, and that's something you better get through your thick brain. Now call your lawyer because last thing I heard he is wondering how the Marshals and the Bureau of Prisons lost track of you."

43

AS RAYNOSA DROVE HIS MONEY-GREEN AVENTADOR IP 700 UNDER THE DAILY CENTER TO PARK IT, Denardo, who was well hidden in the building across the street, watched his every move. He knew that the only way to get to The Devil would be through his lawyer. Perish had set everything up really well with the chiefs, who all seemed to want The Devil dead.

Not only had she had the entire floor wired with Dynamite, but she had Raynosa's office bugged to see if the chiefs had intended to carry out what they had agreed with her to do.

Denardo watched and waited as Raynosa, who had climbed onto the elevator, made his way up to the thirteenth floor to his office.

"One wrong move and everybody goes up in flames," he said to himself as he stared thorough the scope of the high-powered rifle. In the office he could see the chiefs, who all sat around a round table waiting on Lil Devil's lawyer to make his entrance.

"Cynthia, please postpone the rest of my appointments for today until later this week," Raynosa said, going up to the hallway towards his office.

"Yes sir, I already have, and the men who you are about to meet with would have been crowded into your office, so I moved them to the conference room down the hall."

"Thanks."He said, doing an about-face.

He headed down the hall over to the conference room and as his hand touched the doorknob his palm became sweaty.

He turned the knob and made his way into the room, hesitating to stare into the faces of the most powerful men in Chicago.

Without saying a word and with all of the men staring over in his direction, he made his way to the seat at the front of the table and sat down.

"Gentlemen, we all know why we are here today, and we all seem to be reasonable enough to come to terms with reaching the goal we have set to reach. Before I go forth with this meeting I would like to say that I am here on behalf of my client as well as myself."

"Had you been here on behalf of your client, I'm sure this whole office would have blown up the moment we walked into it," a well-dressed, short Spanish man who went by the name Dizzy Gardona said, making the other six men in the room laugh.

"Your client has made attempts to have each and every man that sits around this table assassinated and you expect us to trust anything he says?" Cheeko, the prince for the Latin Kings said with a frown.

"Look gentlemen, I know you all feel as if my client The Devil is not to be trusted, but I'm assuring you that he wants a cease fire as well as any of you."

"So why the hell is he still having his Disciples shoot up everything we've established every chance he get?" asked M-Jettic, acting Chief for the GDs.

"My client is not only one that's doing the killing in the city and he's definitely not the only one that has almost been assassinated."

"Well it sure as hell wasn't due to us attempting to hit him," M-Jettic said, raising his voice.

"Unlike your client, the men at this table have enough respect for each other to still let each other know when someone so high on the ladder will be hit. We all have renegades in our crews, and those hits none of us can be held accountable for, but I assure you counselor, none of us ordered any hits on your client, although it is more than warranted."

Raynosa wiped the sweat from his forehead and undid his tie.

"Look, this is the proposal that my client is putting forth here today. He wants you men to drop the five and six-point stars. He wants to reunite all the gangs under the seven-point star which he and his deceased father founded."

"We do that, we make him the King of All Kings, meaning he will be over the top of all of us, so Hell No!" Ratcho, the Chief of the Vice Lords, said in disgust.

"As far as my client is concerned this is not something that can be negotiated. He has said that if you refuse to willfully allow him to sit on top of you all, he will put every man in this room under the dirt and then he'll stand over the top of you all"

Upon hearing this all then men broke out in an uproar while talking at the same time.

Denardo, who was listening on, knew that none of the men had any intention to do as Perrish had gotten them to agree to do. Besides, these were the same men who were responsible for his Aunt Sandy's death as far as he was concerned.

He picked up his phone, dialed out and on the second ring Perrish answered.

"Hello?"

"These guys aren't budging; they are stuck on their own agendas."

"Well, send them to hell!" she said, hanging up.

Denardo rose to his feet while removing the trigger to the explosives from his pocket. He then hit the red button and watched as the entire thirteenth floor blow up.

44

"**DO YOU THINK ANYONE WILL NOTICE THAT ALL OF THE CHIEFS AND PRINCES JUST GOT BLOWN TO BITS?**" Denardo asked moving up behind Perrish who he scooped up into his arms, causing her to smile.

"I know one person in particular who definitely will notice that they all are gone," she said, turning to face him. She kissed him, and then placed her head to his chest.

"I sure would hate to be on the other side of your fury," he said, kissing her gently upon her forehead.

"Now that Ayana is safely out of the city and in New York with your mother we can finish this and be on with our lives."

"Whatever you say, Angel of mine whatever you say."

"Come on, it's only one last person to eliminate," she said, taking his hand while leading him over towards the door.

45

NOW THAT ALL HIS RIVALS HAD BEEN ELIMINATED, it should have been easy for The Devil to relax, but now he had even more to worry about than before.

Without their Chiefs, Ahks and Princes to control them, the gangsters had all became renegades and were refusing to go back to taking orders from anyone outside of themselves. He was now not just the most feared man in all of Chicago, but he was the most hated. He had no idea that many of the people loved the Chiefs they had served for many years. As he sat in the dimly lit mansion he began to think of how powerless he really was. He needed to reassure himself that he was the Kings of Kings now that all the other powerful men who opposed him were eliminated.

He rose to his feet, hovering over the thirty man entourage that followed him everywhere he went by a distance of least two and a half feet. As he walked they all walked with him making sure no one got near him. The men traveled across the first floor over to the door where they exited.

The Devil looked over the small army of men that surrounded his entire compound. He made his way down the steps towards the blue and grey Bugatti at the foot of the steps awaiting him. As the back door opened a familiar face appeared, causing The Devil to stop dead in his tracks.

Perrish stepped out of the car holding a Ruger 9-millimeter which she pointed straight at his chest.

"Kill her!" he yelled to his men but they didn't budge.

She raised her weapon towards his head, and then fired three shots which caught him in the upper torso.

He looked at her with a confused look on his face as he staggered back and fell upon the steps.

She walked over to where he lay and as he looked up at her she placed the gun to his forehead and pulled the trigger, blowing his brains out from the back of his head. She then turned and when she did she saw all of the Disciples kneeling down, bowing to her while holding up the seven-point star.

Denardo got out of the car walked over to where Perrish stood. She held the gun smoking by her side; he hugged her, removing the murder weapon from her hands.

They both got back into the car and the driver pulled off slowly as the Disciples continued to bow in her presence.

IF YOU COULD IMAGINE, TONY "SCARFACE" MONTANA, having a son then you can imagine the ride that you're about to be taken on when you read **ARISING OF A LEGENDARY SON**.

MIGUEL CASTRO who had no idea of his father's true identity, is about to find out that he is the son of the most powerful Drug Lord in the history of America.

After being raised as a peasant in the jungles of Venezuela with his mother, he returns to the United States and upon using his deceased father's passport, he is arrested and jailed under the suspicion that he, himself is Razor Wire Castro or Bloody Castro as his father was known.

His mother who has been trying to shield him from the life style his father ruled over will now be forced to tell her son the truth. The truth alienated mother and son; Miguel resented his mother for holding back the truth about his father, which sends him on a mission to claim his place as heir to the throne. He will become a man that even his late father would have feared.

The young Castro links up with local up and coming gangsters in the United States, who he meets while in the juvenile center and creates a criminal organization that becomes more powerful than any that has ever been seen before.

With the help of his Venezuelan father in law and his homeboy he met while in the juvenile center who is a drug smuggler for a Mexican Cartel, Miguel Castro will take the under world by storm.

Not even the finest team of ATF, FBI or DEA agents will be able to stop his reign.

See what happens when a boy who is forced to grow up fast surpasses even his father's legacy, becoming the biggest drug lord in America, Mexico and Venezuela.

HERE'S A SNEAK PEEK INTO "ARISING OF A LEGENDARY SON"!

What had seemed to be an eternity, which was actually no more than eighteen years, had finally passed, now being able to see the great city of New York again brought back memories that she thought had been erased from her mind forever. As the chilling winter air tore away at her trenched grey wool pea coat her son Miguel, who had never seen the states, stood behind her and embraced her tightly in his arms causing her to smile.

"America Momma?" He asked, staring over at the massive steel structure that made up the Statue of Liberty.

"Yes, Miguel, this is the United States of America, the home of the free and the land of the brave."

She marveled at the skyline that was adorned by beautiful buildings, some were familiar and others newly built. Even though so much bad had taken place in and around this great city, she still loved it. The sound of a horn blared through the air as the captain's voice came over the loud speakers.

"Ladies and gentlemen, please gather your belongings and exit on your right out onto the deck of the ship, we will soon be docking,"

"Welcome to the United States of America!"

Miguel and his mother Silia Castro walked towards the front of the ship as hundreds of passengers made their way towards them.

"Here hold onto to this." She said handing him a United States passport that he opened up. Inside of it was a picture of a man that he had never seen before in his life.

"Momma is this my picture he asked?"

Silia looked at her seventeen year old son in the eyes and said,

"It is your father."

Miguel, who couldn't get his mother to ever say more than five words about his father, closed the passport. He knew nothing about his father except that he had ran off and left his mother when she was pregnant and judging from what his mother had told him about the man he was glad that they never met. His dad was a bum that he would never have claimed anyways, so his self-exile out of their lives was best.

As the ship came upon the port, ropes were tossed overboard and men on the docks quickly tied them to make sure that the ship did not drift back out into the sea. A side door on the ship was opened and like ants, the people aboard, exited the ship heading down towards customs where security booths were set up. There was a very pretty black woman with light grey eyes that stood awaiting them.

"Your Passports or Visas!" The woman said reaching her hand out to take their traveling papers.

After fumbling through her purse as if she had no idea where their passports were, Silia pulled the small booklet from her bag and handed it over to the woman. The TSA Agent scanned the passport while looking over at the computer screen in front of her.

"Welcome home Ma'am." The woman said smiling at Silia as she handed her back her passport and motioned her through the metal detector.

Once on the other side of the metal detector, Silvia turned around and waited on Miguel as the woman scanned the passport of her husband. The TSA Agent smiled at Miguel, but he could sense that something was wrong by how long she was taking to allow him to pass the security point. Seven USA Customs Agents surrounded the booth where Miguel stood and as soon as Silia seen them her heart dropped into her stomach.

"Sir come with us," a clean shaved black man that wore a nice tailored suit said taking a hold of Miguel's arm.

"Where are you taking him?" Silia asked, as she attempted to approach the booth.

Two other agents quickly stopped her.

"Mrs. Castro, your husband is wanted by the government of The United States for several crimes."

"No! No! You're making a mistake. He is not my husband, this is my son!" She said screaming to the top of her lungs which caused the huge crowd of spectators who were already looking on to begin to pay more attention to the situation.

The agents escorted Miguel to a well secured part of the establishment heading down a hallway which leads them into an office like setting. They opened a door to one of the offices and took Miguel inside, where three more men, who were FBI, DEA and ATF agents were seated around a table.

Mrs. Castro who was screaming and fighting the customs agents in order to get to Miguel was allowed to enter the room.

"We've been after you for a very long time Sir!" The FBI agent who sat at the table in front of Miguel said as he opened up a folder that sat on the table in front of him.

"For what?" Miguel asked looking down at the FBI agent whose name was Diaz.

"For conspiracy, running a continuing criminal enterprise, the Rico statue, and several dozen murders of civilians, police officers and politicians. Importing and trafficking every drug known to the American streets Castro, and more. Look, we know exactly who you are, but it seems that you want to play games with us Mr. Castro. Mr. Miguel Razor wires Castro. Murderous Castro, Bloody

Castro or whatever other name you are known by in the underworld."

"I've never even been to your country to have committed any crimes against it so you are mistaken." Miguel said looking around the room at the other agents with hate in his blood shot eyes."

"This is a mistake! Silia said crying. This is my son, not my husband. Just as he has said, he has never been to this country! He was born in Europe and raised in Venezuela, she said placing her hands over her face to cover it. My son is only seventeen years old and he has no proper traveling documents so I used his father's passport to get him into the country. This is all my fault so arrest me and let my son go."

All of the agents in the room began to look around at each other.

"What if she's telling the truth Diaz? Agent Blake the DEA Agent said.

"Yeah look at the guy, the Castro we are looking for is more than sixty years old. This fella doesn't look a day over fifteen." Agent Marquise the ATF Agent said.

"Well, well still have to check it out. Well send him over to the juvenile wing of Riker's Island until I talk to supervising agent Marco." Diaz said while standing.

As they began escorting him from the room Miguel turned back to look at his mother. The look he gave her was one that crushed her heart. It was a look of betrayal and hate. A look that her late husband had given her the night she had told him that she had received news from her doctor that she was unable to bare him a child...

The Author, Kingdawud Mujahid Burgess, is no stranger to poverty, prisons, peril, or pain. Through true life experiences he knows first hand what its like to be shot, stabbed, have to kill or be killed. Based on the journey he has taken in life, he is able to tell us about a world many of us wouldn't dare to venture into... A world that has left generation after generation scared for life, dead, incarcerated or turned out on medication.

At the tender age of ten upon his mother's death, he to became a victim of the perils of poverty and pistols. With no job experience and not wanting to remain homeless or starve, he chose to sell drugs as a way to escape his environment and its hellish conditions. This lead to his federal incarceration of 200 months as well as a two year juvenile sentence and a six year state sentence.

Due to his anger and attitude of refusing to go for anything from anybody; he spent most of his time in solitude where a man is able to find out very quickly who he is and about the world around him. He came to understand that everything this world possesses that is most precious has to be found in the deepest and darkest corners of the earth, that many men wish and will never choose to travel to. It is through his writing that we are able to get a glimpse of hell without having to ourselves feel the sting of its flames. Kingdawud who is nearly finished serving his entire 16 year and 8 month federal sentence spends his time reading, writing and learning about the world.